A
Disconcerting Concert

by
Richard S. Howland

A Disconcerting Concert

ISBN: 978-0-9893037-2-9

This is a work of fiction. The characters and events in this novel are creations of the author's imagination, and the reader should not assume any connections to living people, actual institutions or real events.

Thank you to Jane Schock for her precise proofreading.

Book design and production by Kate Weisel,
Bellingham, WA (weiselcreative.com)

Cover illustrations:
Bellingham Bay photo – Kate Weisel
Keyboard: viperagp – Fotolia
Motorcycle: Skovoroda – Fotolia

Glass-eyed mice
Have made a nest in my piano.
I mark the un-tolled hours
In a round of notes,
Driving death away.

— Gian-Carlo Menotti (1911-2007)

Cast of Characters

Helen Alexander: former UW basketball player
Johnny Alexander: adult son of Helen
Abigail Baker: ex-girlfriend of Steven Ostrander
Bobby Baldovino: chimpanzee center volunteer
Red Banks: friend of Dirk
Rory Bliss: pianist
Isaac Casey: friend of Dirk
Paul Cronn: caretaker at Bay Horizon Park
Lt. Ed Davis: sheriff's detective
Kay Day: friend of Steve Ostrander
Marcus Perfecto-Gomez: slack line athlete
Dirk Hollinger: publicity chair for the musical
    society
Josephine Hurt: resident of Yew Rock Mobile
    Home Park
Mary Locke: president, Whatcom Musical
    Society
Mac Martino: friend and neighbor of Dirk
    Hollinger
Saundra Miller: violinist
Adrian Mondragon: Musical Society treasurer
Steven Ostrander: student and page turner
Leslie Quarles: attorney
Frank Speaker: retired opera professor

Chapter 1

Men in their 40s and 50s wore leather. Women in their 70s and 80s were dressed in wool. About 200 people had squeezed into a concert hall that actually was a motorcycle repair shop.

Adrian Mondragon, treasurer of the Whatcom Musical Society, was living his dream of holding a classical concert at Mondragon Motorcycles, where he repaired Harleys and he rehabilitated pianos. Adrian had arranged for a nationally known violinist and pianist to perform with a Baldwin grand piano that Adrian had painstakingly restored. Dirk Hollinger, volunteer publicity chair for the society, had publicized the recital not only in the local news and entertainment publications, but also in a regional motorcycle magazine.

Helpers had rolled all of the motorcycles out of the shop to make room for folding chairs. In consideration of the silver-haired ladies, the concert could not be too long because of those hard chairs. Mondragon also wanted his motorcycles to be back inside the shop before dark.

One motorcyclist sat directly in front of Dirk. This cyclist evidently was trying to look tough in his leather and denim outfit, thought Hollinger. But the cyclist had a soft face and delicate hands. He also wore a black skull cap, an earring, glasses and a mousey beard. With his leather vest hanging over the back of his chair, he displayed an orange shirt bearing an advertisement on the back for a Harley-Davidson shop in Squamish, British Columbia, not far across the Canadian border from Whatcom County, which was as far north as you could go in northwest Washington State.

The first piece listed in the printed program was the world premier of *Rigoletto's Regret*, composed by Alexandra Diggs, a professor at Western Washington University in Bellingham.

Before the music began, Red Banks cautioned his friend Dirk not to expect too much in a world premier.

"I could write a sloppy piece and invite my neighbors over for a barbecue, and call it a world premier," Red, sitting next to Dirk, remarked. "This one could be just *Rigoletto* regurgitated."

When they finished the new piece, violinist Saundra Miller and pianist Rory Bliss left the stage, but a young page turner for the pianist remained seated on stage until Mondragon beckoned him to go behind the makeshift curtains to an office that served as backstage. The audience chuckled indulgently at this misstep.

Mondragon had asked a slightly built student at Western Washington University to turn the pages of the musical scores for Bliss. Dirk knew nothing more about the youth. The page turner had blond hair that was longer than Saundra Miller's blonde hair. Dirk wondered why Frank Speaker was not turning pages today. Speaker was a retired opera professor who often served as page turner for piano players at concerts sponsored by the Whatcom Musical Society.

The two musicians and the young page turner reappeared on stage shortly and resumed their performance. After each piece, the two musicians bowed and left the stage, along with the page turner, who now was on the same page as the two musicians in regard to exits and entrances.

The second piece performed by Miller and Bliss was *Shade* by Richard Barrett, who was born in 1959. Dirk thought Shade was interesting but a shade too modern and cacophonous.

Next on the program was *Poeme for Violin and Orchestra*, Op. 25, by Ernest Chausson (1855-1899). A friend of Debussy, Chausson wrote one published opera, one symphony and several chamber works, according to the program notes. Violinists loved his *Poeme* (1896). He died when he lost control of a bicycle going downhill. Perhaps this factoid might serve as a cautionary note to the motorcyclists in the audience.

Now Bliss performed solo, playing Nancarrow's six-minute "Canon for Ursula No. 1," from Three *Canons for Ursula* (1989). First, Bliss spoke to the audience about the piano compositions of Conlon Nancarrow (1912-1997). Born in Arkansas, he became a Communist and fought against Franco. He moved to Mexico in 1940 to escape official harassment in the United States directed at Communist veterans of the Spanish Civil War. In Mexico he wrote music for mechanical player pianos, which could produce complex rhythms faster than humans could. He was influenced by Arnold Schoenberg and John Cage, yet Dirk found his music to be much more pleasant than their music. In 1982, Nancarrow won a MacArthur Award, which paid him $300,000 across five years. Music lovers began to take notice of him, and encouraged him to write music that human beings could play.

Next was *Sonata in E b Major for Piano and Violin*, Op. 12, No. 3, by Beethoven, followed by "Allegro vivo," "Intermede" and "Finale" from *Sonata for violin and piano in G major* by Debussy. This was the last piece performed by Debussy on piano, in 1917, prior to his death in 1918 of cancer.

After a standing ovation, the encore was *Mercy* by Max Richter.

A man behind Dirk shouted "Bravo!" for the third or fourth time.

Red Banks complained quietly to Dirk: "I guess he only liked the pianist and not the violinist, because 'bravo' is the masculine form."

Red, a retired court stenographer who held a degree in linguistics, went on to explain that in Italian "brava" is the feminine form; "bravi" is plural for two or more men, or multiple men and women; "brave" is for two or more women.

As they discussed the concert on their way out of the motorcycle shop, Red said Bliss was a competent pianist. Miller, he added, was a skillful violinist and was comfortable in front of an audience, but Red thought Miller possessed a less than topnotch violin.

Throughout the concert, Miller had been calm, collected, and slightly cool.

"These qualities work well in some repertoire," Red postulated, "but a lot of violin repertoire needs temperament and passion, and I couldn't tell from her playing tonight how much of those qualities she brings to the fingerboard."

Dirk thought the pianist had played too loudly at times, drowning out Miller's light plucking. But overall it had been an excellent show. Miller, an attractive woman in her 30s, had worn a low-cut dress, exposing much of her torso. Dirk wondered why male classical musicians seemed usually to strait-jacket themselves in formal wear when they performed.

Red replied, "Why do female musicians do their striptease? Probably because the majority of male concert goers are still straight, and a revealing gown is a good tonic for helping them to digest classical music. But women should not complain about feeling underappreciated for their real artistic quality when they encourage the audience to notice their gowns even before the first note is heard."

Dirk said goodnight to Red. Then he went looking for the pianist Bliss in the motorcycle shop's office. Dirk had volunteered his home as lodgings for Bliss. The violinist was staying at the lake-view home of the society's president. Miller and Bliss had arrived last night and would leave tomorrow morning.

While looking for Bliss, Dirk noticed that Frank Speaker, the frequent page turner who had been replaced today by the young man, was talking quietly to the motorcyclist with the orange shirt bearing the name of the shop in Squamish, B.C.

Speaker often wore a wooden bow tie to concerts, and he wore one now. The ties were made by hand by a father-son team in Burnaby, British Columbia, just across the Canadian border from Bellingham. The ties were fashioned from maple and walnut reclaimed from remnants at a lumber mill in Oregon, burnished with Swedish teak oil and Israeli leather neck straps. Dirk thought these ornaments were somewhat ostentatious.

As Dirk drove home with Bliss, the pianist complained about his previous lodging in Missoula, Montana, a town similar to Bellingham, Washington, in that both cities were arts-oriented college towns with about 60,000 to 80,000 residents.

After his concert in Missoula, the pianist spent the night as the guest of a concert organizer whose home also housed a huge dog. The hosts swore that their Saint Bernard never entered the guest bedroom. But dog hairs floated into the guest room through the heating vents. They infiltrated the sheets and blankets of the guest bed, probably via the washing machine and clothes dryer.

"It's a relief to be in Bellingham tonight," Bliss told Dirk.

Dirk lived in a mobile home, and he had hesitated to offer his extra bedroom to a traveling musician, due to the less than glamorous image of mobile homes. But most people did not realize how comfortable modern mobile homes could be. On the inside, with cathedral ceilings, picture windows and modern drywall, you easily could forget that you were in a mobile home.

Bliss still was talking about the Saint Bernard in Missoula, whose name was Thor.

"Thor seemed to accept houseguests, as long as one stayed away from his resting spots. There was a blanket on the floor of the living room where he would lie. There was another blanket on the sofa in the TV room, and the blanket was his territory, too."

Thor had an enlarged heart and lost consciousness on occasion. Consequently, someone had to be with Thor at all times. Bliss's hosts planned their entire lives around Thor. They also constantly petted the dog and reassured him. Thor drooled a lot.

"Sometimes the wife or the husband wiped the dog's mouth, and sometimes the saliva dripped onto the floor," Bliss recalled.

"I took off my socks and noticed how filthy they were, from walking on the linoleum floor. From then on, I wore my shoes in the house. It must be difficult to keep the floors clean in a house with a huge slobbering dog," Bliss said.

It was widely rumored that Bliss and Miller were lovers. If so, Dirk did not fully appreciate what Miller, a vibrant and personable young woman, saw in Bliss, who seemed to be a rather prissy and self-involved fellow.

"Dogs can be great companions," Dirk said. "Personally I don't really like having them underfoot all the time, but a well trained dog can be a joy. Service dogs are terrific. The problem is that most people don't have the time or self-discipline to train their dogs."

"You can say that again," Bliss agreed. "One can't even go for a walk in a public park without some overexcited canine jumping on your clean pants, even though most parks have leash laws. Dog owners seem to think leash laws do not apply to their precious pets."

"I've heard that some dogs do not react well to leashes. As long as the owner can maintain voice control over the dog, I don't mind."

"Again, it's a matter of training," Bliss said. "But one cannot train a dog not to shed hair. If one lives with a dog, one's house and car will be covered in dog hair."

"In Missoula, there was no carpet — just linoleum," Bliss continued. "There was no waste basket in the guest bedroom. There were no towel bars in the bathrooms. The owners said they thought they would sell the house after remodeling it, and they had left it for the new owners to install the kind of towel bars they wanted. But that was years ago. And one would think the house would have been more attractive to buyers if it already had towel bars."

Dirk tried to recall whether he had emptied the waste baskets in his guest suite.

"What bugs me," Dirk said, "are those towel racks with round edges. I hate it when my towels fall off those things. Every towel bar should have squared edges."

Bliss looked bored.

"Another thing I hate is when people put in the toilet paper so it unrolls from the bottom instead of the top," Dirk offered.

Bliss looked comatose.

Dirk changed the subject.

"How can Saundra remember all the notes without reading the score?" he asked.

"One remembers a piece basically through three of our senses: hearing, sight and touch," Bliss lectured. "One learns and remembers by ear. One visualizes the written music in one's mind. And you remember kinetically, or through what you might call the muscle memory of the fingers. Saundra almost always knows her music by heart by the time she is ready to perform it in public, but an accompanist, if we work with multiple soloists, doesn't have to know every piece by heart, for crying out loud."

Dirk said, "She played some of those notes so fast that she wouldn't have been able to read sheet music fast enough anyway."

Dirk noticed that Bliss' fingernails were cut very close to the skin, and Dirk asked him whether professional musicians often had manicures. He said very few do so. He knew of only one flutist who got a manicure when he was due to perform on television and there would be close-up shots of his fingers.

Bliss looked at Dirk's hands.

"One could not play a violin with nails so long as yours," he said.

Dirk noted that a pianist cannot carry his own instrument around, unlike other musicians. He speculated that the cello might be easier to play than most other instruments because the cello stands on the floor so the musician does not have to hold it up. Bliss agreed that the cello "probably is easier."

Chapter 2

Thirty-six hours later, Lt. Ed Davis of the Whatcom County Sheriff's Department knocked on Dirk's door. Davis and Dirk knew each other from when Dirk was a news reporter for The Bellingham Bugle. Dirk had left the much diminished newspaper to manage Yew Rock Mobile Home Park, which his father owned, on Yew Street just outside the city limits of Bellingham.

Dirk welcomed the lieutenant into his home. The lieutenant did not waste time with small talk.

"Do you know Steven Ostrander?" Davis asked.

Dirk shook his head and said, "No."

"How about Rory Bliss?"

"Sure. He performed for the Whatcom Musical Society this weekend. He spent a couple of nights here with me. I'm the publicity chair for the society, and our board members often take performers into our homes to save on hotel costs."

"Yeah, I've seen your name in the media, announcing this or that activity of the music society. It's why I'm here this morning. Did you see the concert on Saturday?"

"Sure."

"Steven Ostrander was the page turner for Bliss."

"I did not meet him," Dirk said. "Is he in some kind of trouble?"

"You could say that. We found his body yesterday at Bay Horizon Park."

"Good grief. Did he kill himself?"

"Why would you think that?"

"Well, he kind of embarrassed himself during the concert. The violinist and the piano player left the stage after their first piece, but the page turner stayed on stage until someone summoned him. The audience laughed at him as he left the stage. His name was Steve?"

"Steven Ostrander. We think someone killed him and dumped his body at the park."

"I don't know where that park is."

"It's near Birch Bay. We've talked only to his family so far. His sister thinks his death might have something to do with the concert."

"How so?"

"I don't want to go into any details," Lt. Davis said. "But I will tell you this, because I know you, and I trust you not to blab about it. Steve's sister thinks he spent at least part of the night with Saundra Miller."

"That seems like a stretch," Dirk replied. "Saundra is 10 or 15 years older than the page turner. She's an accomplished musician, and he was a novice. What would she see in him?"

"He probably was just a plaything," the lieutenant offered. "Were you with Bliss the whole time?"

It dawned on Dirk that the rumors about Miller and Bliss being at least casual lovers might be true.

"Yeah. I drove him from the concert here to my house. He slept in the guest room. In the morning I served him breakfast and took him to the airport."

"SeaTac Airport?"

"Bellingham Airport. He was going to fly to SeaTac and transfer to a plane to Portland. His next show was in Oregon. He did not have a car at his disposal, so how could he take the body out to Birch Bay?"

"Was Bliss in your guest room all night?"

"As far as I know, he was. I didn't hear him go out or come in."

"Did you sleep through the night or did you get up at all?

"I slept very well," Dirk recalled. "Usually I don't sleep that well when someone I don't really know is spending the night."

"How did you feel in the morning? Could Bliss have slipped a sleeping pill into your nightcap?"

"I don't remember any ill effects. I think it's more likely that the page turner somehow an-tagonized some of the motorcyclists who were at the recital. There were some pretty tough-looking guys. I remember one of them who I could describe in detail, although I have to admit that he was not one of the toughest looking bikers there."

"Those guys mostly are mild-mannered accountants and lawyers during the week, and motorcyclists on weekends," Davis said. "I'd like to see your guest room."

"Be my guest," Dirk replied.

Davis smirked. "I know how you newspaper guys love a pun — any pun."

"Only when we're writing headlines."

Davis looked around the room but found nothing of obvious interest.

"Would you object to a crime-scene team coming here?" the lieutenant asked.

"Not at all."

Chapter 3

After the lieutenant left, Dirk became curious about Bay Horizon Park. He felt that he needed to see the park in order to understand what had happened to the page turner. The crime-scene team would not arrive at Dirk's place for another couple of hours, so he had some free time and he decided to drive out to the park. He found its location online. While on the Internet, he checked the Web site of the Bugle in order to see what the newspaper was reporting so far about the incident at Bay Horizon Park. So far the news was scanty.

He drove north on Interstate 5 and exited to westbound Birch Bay-Lynden Road. Then he drove south on Blaine Road a short distance to Alderson Road, where he turned right and found a sign pointing to Bay Horizon Park.

There was no sign of a police investigation at the park. A few cars were parked in front of a recreation hall, but there did not appear to be many people at the park. The site had served as an Air Force radar station during the Cold War, on the watch for hostile aircraft from across the Pacific Ocean. The Air Force had decommissioned its

Blaine Station in 1979, and Whatcom County had taken over the campus. Several two-story barracks that had housed airmen were still there.

After Dirk had looked around for a while, an older gentleman approached him.

"What is this place?" Dirk asked the man.

"In July and August, it's a camp for kids with special needs," he said. "Each dorm has 47 beds, so we can accommodate as many as 180 people. At other times of the year these buildings are available for conventions. It's not very luxurious, with only a few bathrooms, but we have a tennis court and a two-lane bowling alley. I'm the caretaker. I live here."

"I understand that it used to be an Air Force station," Dirk said.

"Yes, sir. I was stationed here myself in 1967, with the 757th Radar Squadron. Blaine was an ideal assignment in those days, with two big cities nearby: Seattle and Vancouver. Most radar stations were in the middle of nowhere. My cousins lived in Everett, so I spent a lot of weekends with them. Some of the facilities that were here are gone now. The county demolished the steam plant and the big tower. I wish the county would preserve the station as a military museum instead of tearing it down."

"I heard a body was found here yesterday," Dirk said.

"Some kids found the body in that field," the caretaker said, pointing to a large grassy area between the park and Alderson Road.

"The victim was a student in Bellingham. I wonder how he got way out here. Most people in Bellingham don't even know about this place."

"Well, there aren't many people around here this time of year. That field is pretty dark at night. It's as good a place as any to dump a body, I suppose. Maybe now more people will take an interest in this old radar station."

Dirk asked, "Do you have a business card?"

"No, they've never given me business cards."

Dirk pulled out a small notebook from his vest pocket.

"Do you mind giving me your name?" he asked.

"Are you a reporter?"

"No, but I used to be. I might write a freelance magazine piece about this case. If I want to talk to you again, it would be a lot easier to call you than to drive here again."

"I've been wondering when the newspapers and TV stations will send out some reporters," the old man groused. He gave Dirk a phone number and added, "My name is Paul Cronn."

Chapter 4

L ate in the day, Lt. Davis telephoned Dirk.

"I'm going to ask Miller and Bliss to come back to Bellingham so I can talk to them," the lieutenant said. "May I tell them that they are welcome to stay where they stayed before?"

"You want Bliss to stay at my place and Miller to stay at the club president's house?"

"Exactly. Of course they could stay at a hotel if they choose. I just want them to feel like they're guests in our town and not necessarily suspects."

"But they are suspects," Dirk noted. "They could be dangerous."

"They will know that law enforcement is watching them. And they have no motive to harm you or the club president."

Dirk was intrigued by the investigation, and he wanted to help the Sheriff's Department. He agreed to try to persuade the club president to go along.

"One thing I can't picture, though, is that Bliss or Miller would know anything about Bay Horizon Park," Dirk commented. "Even people from Bellingham don't ordinarily go there."

"Anyone could find it on Google Maps or GPS," Davis countered.

Dirk called Mary Locke, president of the Whatcom Musical Society. He argued that the society needed to protect its reputation by helping the police to find out who killed Steven Ostrander. Mary said she was certain that Saundra Miller could not possibly be involved in the killing, and Mary would be delighted to enjoy Saundra's company again. She said she would ask the board members to permit the society to pay for Bliss and Miller's travel expenses.

"We need to stay on good terms with them so they will perform for us again in the future," Mary declared. "I wonder whether they will want legal advice. They probably have their own attorneys for business affairs, but they might appreciate a local criminal attorney. I will ask Leslie Quarles to step up on a pro bono basis."

Quarles, an assistant attorney general for Washington State who was based in Bellingham, was a member of the Whatcom Musical Society.

Miller and Bliss had a short hiatus in their concert schedule in mid-week, so they returned to Bellingham promptly. They arrived at Bellingham Airport together aboard the same flight. Mary Locke and Dirk were there to greet them and to chauffeur the musicians separately according to their various schedules and desires.

Before they had left the airport grounds, Bliss told Dirk that no one should think Bliss might have been involved in a love triangle with Miller and the page turner.

"If I wanted to kill anyone, it would be that stupid great Dane in Missoula," Bliss insisted. "He was far more annoying than the page turner in Bellingham. Saundra has her little flings all over the country. I don't care. She and I had our fun, but that was a long time ago. Her boy toys are nothing to me — especially a page turner. One really doesn't pay much attention to a page turner. There might not even be any page turners in the near future. Pianists are starting to read from a laptop or an iPad while performing. They can turn a page with the flick of a wrist or a tap on a foot pedal. The thought of murdering a page turner — such nonsense really can aggravate you if one is willing to waste time thinking about it."

"I told Lt. Davis that I did not hear you leave or come back during that night," Dirk offered. "The police searched the room where you stayed and found nothing to tie you to Steven Ostrander."

"Of course they found nothing. And they won't," Bliss insisted.

"How do you pick a page turner?" Dirk asked.

"Whoever is producing the show usually handles that sort of chore," Bliss answered. "There are some semi-professional page turners who do it a lot. Sometimes a fellow pianist will do it, which probably is the best solution, because he or she likely will know the music and will know intuitively when to turn the page. More often one gets stuck with a stage hand who happens to know how to read music, or maybe whichever stage hand is wearing the nicest clothes.

"As a page turner, one gets an excellent seat for seeing and hearing the performance, but it's a stressful job," Bliss continued. "One surely will be literally red-faced if one drops the score or knocks the pianist off his seat. One absolutely must turn pages at the top of the page — never from the bottom. If the audience pays any attention to the page turner, the page turner has done a poor job.

"However, there is a piece that elevates the page turner to the status of performer. It's called Trio for Flute, Piano and Page Turner, if you can believe that. The composer calls upon the page turner to hold down some of the keys of the piano and to fiddle with the innards of the instrument. I have not performed that piece of piddle."

Bliss now complained about some of the publicity that had preceded his performance with Sandra Miller in Bellingham, and some of the wording in the programs that club members had handed out at the concert.

"Saundra and I should be billed equally. That means my title should be 'pianist,' not piano accompanist. Saundra played some solo pieces, so she was not 'accompanied' all the time, and I played a solo piece, so I was not just an accompanist, but a pianist in my own right. It's important not to give a professional musician a title that minimizes his or her role.

"In the future, please be sure you list performers as: violinist Jane Smith and pianist John Jones, or Jane Smith on violin and John Jones on piano. 'With' instead of 'and' would emphasize the partnership and collaboration. Both 'and' and 'with' are acceptable."

After Bliss settled into the guest room again, Dirk drove him to the Sheriff's Department in downtown Bellingham. On the way, Dirk played a tape of an orchestra performing *Butterfly Lovers*, a concerto written in China in 1958 by Cheng Gang and He Zhanhao for Western-style orchestras. The piece was censored by the Chinese government until after the Cultural Revolution of the 1960s and '70s. Dirk had heard the concerto live years ago in San Francisco, where the orchestra had employed a few traditional Chinese instruments, including a five-string pipa. Dirk's recording by the Central Philharmonic Orchestra of China featured a violin instead of a pipa.

Bliss knew nothing of *Butterfly Lovers*. He liked the piece at first. He said the orchestration was clever. Eventually, however, he tired of the pentatonic or five-note scale. European classical music has a seven-note scale. Ultimately, *Butterfly Lovers* just was too long for Bliss.

They parked near a dawn redwood tree that Dirk always had considered remarkable. Unlike the redwoods of California, this one was deciduous and lost its leaves during the winter. They had a few minutes before the appointment with Lt.

Davis, so Dirk pointed out a plaque beside the tree.

Scientists had thought the dawn redwood was extinct, known only from fossils, until some living trees were found in China in the 1940s. A Bellingham resident obtained seeds and planted a dawn redwood at the courthouse in 1953. In 1990, the county was going to cut down the redwood in order to make way for rebuilding the courthouse, but the plans were altered and the tree was saved.

"It's a nice tree but one couldn't make a piano out of it," Bliss remarked.

"What kind of wood do they use in pianos?" Dirk asked.

"Hard maple, beech, spruce — sometimes plywood," Bliss answered. "Even from the same species of tree, the wood is slightly different due to many factors: microclimate, age and so forth. Every piano has its own personality. Pianists in an area are on a first-name basis with the available pianos, whether the piano is from a performing arts center, a university, a church or a musical rental store. Indeed, there are more good piano players than there are good pianos."

"For your show, we rented a piano from a company in Bellevue, near Seattle," Dirk said.

"One never calls it a 'show' in classical music," Bliss corrected Dirk. "Call it a 'concert' or a 'recital,' please."

Dirk waited outside Lt. Davis' office while the lieutenant interviewed Bliss. As they walked out of the sheriff's headquarters, Bliss complained about the representation that the Music Society had provided him.

"She acted like she was on the lieutenant's team," Bliss said.

"Well, I suppose Leslie Quarles knows Lt. Davis pretty well," Dirk replied. "She is an assistant attorney general, after all. She's a prosecutor, not really a defense attorney."

"If I have to submit to any more questioning, I'm going to find my own attorney," Bliss declared.

They walked to Dirk's vehicle and he drove his houseguest back to Yew Rock Mobile Home Park for the night.

"I don't think I've been to a city of such modest size that has such illogical and confusing streets," Bliss remarked. "One sees so many diagonals and dead-ends."

Dirk knew that newcomers found Bellingham's street grid to be a puzzle. From the mobile home park they had driven north on Yew Street Road, which became just plain Yew Street when it entered Bellingham city limits. They had turned left on Lakeway Drive and had gone west to Ellis Street, where two-way Lakeway veered to the right at a 45-degree angle and became one-way Holly Street. Then they made another 45-degree turn onto two-way Prospect. The courthouse was at Prospect and Central, just south of where Prospect made another 45-degree twist and became DuPont Street.

On the way back to Yew Rock Mobile Home Park, they took Grand Avenue south to Champion Street, where two-way Grand made a 45-degree turn and became one-way Magnolia. At Magnolia they did another 45-degree twist onto two-way Ellis, and turned left onto Lakeway.

"It's because there were three different towns here in the pioneer days," Dirk tried to explain. "Each town faced Bellingham Bay from a different direction because the shore curves. So each town's street grid was at an angle to the grids of the other towns. Eventually they all merged and became one city called Bellingham.

"Another factor is all the creeks, ponds and lakes that interrupt the grid," he added.

"Bellingham is almost as impossible as London, where few streets go more than a block or two without changing name and direction," Bliss commented. "The only way to navigate London is via the underground trains, on foot or by taxi."

Dirk recalled reading a recent article in the New York Times that described the streets of London as "the cardiovascular system of a monster."

It occurred to Dirk that it was very unlikely that Bliss could have found his way around Bellingham well enough to locate Steven Ostrander in the dark of night, even with the help of GPS. And Yew Rock Mobile Home Park was too far from the university campus to walk there.

They entered the park. Before they got from

Dirk's car to the front door, a neighbor waylaid them.

"Oh, Mr. Bliss, would you be so kind as to sign my concert program?" said Josephine Hurt, one of Dirk's immediate neighbors. "I would be so thrilled."

She handed Bliss a pen and her program, and the pianist signed his autograph.

"Our book club meets at 4:30 this afternoon, Mr. Bliss," Josephine noted. "We will discuss *Bel Canto* by Ann Pachett. Have you read it? We'd love to have you join us. It's about a soprano who is held hostage by revolutionaries in South America."

"I have read it," Bliss responded. "Indeed I read it while on tour in South America. Perhaps you are too kind in calling them revolutionaries. They could also be considered terrorists."

"That's just the kind of thing we will discuss. I know our understanding of the book would bene-fit from your professional expertise. Please do join us."

"Maybe Dirk will bring me around to your place at 4:30," Bliss said noncommittally.

When they were inside Dirk's home, Bliss said: "She probably thinks my signature will be valu-able if I'm convicted of murder."

"Oh, I imagine she thinks you're signature is intrinsically valuable. So what do you want to do about the book club?" Dirk asked.

"Oh, I've nothing better to do. One should min-gle with the fans from time to time."

"Josephine has a baby grand piano," Dirk cautioned. "She might ask you to play it."

"Oh, one usually can satisfy the rabble by playing some trifle. It's no trouble."

Josephine and her book club members were from all appearances thrilled to see Bliss and Dirk at the door for the book discussion.

Josephine introduced Patchett's novel by setting the scene. In the opening pages the founder and chairman of an electronics corporation in Japan visited South America to hear lyric soprano Roxane Coss sing, with an accompanist on piano, during a private performance in the home of a national elected official. During the recital, the power went out and gunmen stormed into the palace. A long stand-off with police and armed forces ensued, during which hostages and captors formed close bonds despite their vast cultural differences. The soprano and the businessman fell in love.

Katsumi Hosokawa, the electronics executive, had heard his first opera, *Rigoletto*, when he was 11 years old. For the rest of his life, Hosokawa believed "that life, true life, was something that was stored in music."

Josephine opened the floor for discussion. Dirk had never known any of these book club members to be shy, but all held back. Josephine looked directly at Rory Bliss.

"Music is my career and my consolation," Bliss declared. "I definitely can identify with these two characters in *Bel Canto*."

"Music is what keeps me breathing," said one club member.

"We all need music," said another club member.

"Music is indispensable," agreed a third member. "Life would be so much sadder without music."

Josephine read another quotation from the novel.

" 'Maybe music could be transferred, devoured, owned?' Does anyone think so?"

Again they all waited for Bliss to comment first.

"Certainly music can be transferred and devoured," he said. "In a legal sense a specific piece of music of course can be owned for a few years until the copyright expires. And one can buy music. One can commission music. But without purchasing anything you own any music that you love."

Dirk had read the book, but he stayed quiet for most of the evening. He was thankful that no one mentioned how, in the book, the accompanist had been secretly in love with the soprano. Perhaps the accompanist in the book was jealous of the Japanese businessman, and perhaps Bliss, despite his denials, was jealous of Saundra Miller.

Josephine did ask Bliss to play her piano. He obliged with Nocturne in D-flat major from *Prelude and Nocturne for Left Hand, Op. 9*, by Alexander Scriabin, which Bliss said he was practicing for an upcoming performance in commemoration of the 100th anniversary of the Russian composer's death.

Bliss was in a good mood as he and Dirk returned to Dirk's home. He and Miller would fly out of Bellingham in the morning.

"One finds this sort of thing rather invigorating with the right group of people," he said. "You want them to be respectful, but not too much in awe. You want them to be intelligent but not pedantic."

"Was Josephine's piano adequate?" Dirk asked.

"Yes, it was adequate. Not magnificent, mind you. But one would think she must have had a capable piano tuner here recently."

"Yes, she hires a blind tuner in Mount Vernon, the next city to the south of here," Dirk said. "He lost his eyesight as a teenager. He has a driver who takes him on his rounds."

"Yes, blind piano tuners are fairly common," Bliss remarked. "Their sense of hearing is acute. But it's getting harder to find a tuner. It was a craft that was handed down from father to son, but not so many sons are interested anymore. Most tuners are in their 50s or 60s now. One wonders whether classical music will hang on."

"Josephine's tuner prefers jazz," Dirk noted.

"Jazz is OK, albeit a little too unstructured."

"I've been wondering," Dirk said. "What is the most correct pronunciation of pianist?"

Bliss said he preferred "pee AN ist" with the emphasis on the middle syllable, in line with "vio LIN ist" and "vi OHL ist." He thought it was pretentious to say "PEE an ist."

Chapter 5

Mary Locke, president of the Whatcom Musical Society, hosted a reception at her home following Steven Ostrander's funeral. As a teenager Mary had worked for her father, who manufactured hunting rifles in Iowa. She now delivered food to shut-ins through the Food Samaritans. Like LBJ, she was a "guns and butter" president, strong on defense and strong on social programs. She also volunteered at the Bellingham Senior Center, helping out at the information desk, hosting dances and staffing blood-pressure clinics. She had contributed more than 500 hours of volunteer labor in just one calendar year.

Her intent in holding a reception in honor of Steven Ostrander was to maintain close relations with the Music Department at Western Washington University. Although no one from Ostrander's family was at the reception, many music majors and faculty members were.

At the reception Dirk zeroed in on Adrian Mondragon, treasurer of the music society, who had organized the fateful concert at his motorcycle shop.

"How well do you know those motorcyclists who showed up at the recital?" Dirk asked. "Do you think it's possible that any of them might have killed Steve Ostrander?"

"I know most of them pretty well," Adrian responded. "They're professional people: doctors, lawyers, accountants. They're not criminals."

"But you don't know all of them, do you. There must have been some bikers who don't live in Bellingham, who saw the concert announcement in a motorcycle magazine."

"Sure, there were a few. But motorcycle gang members are not going to be interested in classical music, for crying out loud. I'm sure that even the guys I did not know are doctors, lawyers and accountants, not criminals."

Dirk next chatted briefly with Professor Maurice Tallman, who was standing beside Violet Hardcastle, a librarian at Western Washington. In her 30s with glasses and an old-fashioned hairstyle erected around a prim bun, she was scholarly, yet slender and curvaceous. Tallman served as a volunteer liaison between the university and the music club. Dirk had met Tallman several times, always on campus.

Tonight the professor was regaling the librarian with details about several exceptional photographs on the walls of Mary Locke's home. One photograph, a silver bromide print by Adelaide Hanscom Leeson, depicted a woman sitting atop a large sphere, holding a large tilted bowl from which flowed an ethereal substance that appeared to be bubbles. The photographer evidently had employed multiple exposures in order to achieve astonishing results. Professor Tallman said Adelaide Hanscom settled in Seattle after her studio in San Francisco burned down in the aftermath of the great earthquake of 1906.

"That earthquake was a boon for Bellingham," Violet Hardcastle interjected. "San Francisco needed to rebuild, and Bellingham had plenty of lumber to ship there."

At the time of the fire, Hanscom already was known for her groundbreaking contributions to one of the earliest American books to feature photography as fine art. In Seattle she married Arthur Leeson. In 1909 she upended the traditional motif of mother and child in photographs of the day by photographing a memorable portrait of her husband and their baby son. Leeson died in World War I. Adelaide became depressed, tried to kill herself and died in a hit-and-run car accident in the early 1930s.

But Dirk was more interested in talking with the students who had known Steven Ostrander. He made a point of introducing himself to as many students as he could.

His first two targets were sitting near a picture window overlooking Lake Whatcom. Their names were Christopher Limbson and Amanda Carr. They were sampling the quiche that Mary Locke had prepared for the reception: a salmon quiche and a spinach quiche.

"Real men don't eat quiche," Christopher quipped.

"I would think that real men would eat any-thing and everything," Amanda remarked.

Christopher was friendly and articulate, and seemed like a leader. He grew up in eastern Washington, and graduated from a high school in Coleville. He had lived in Bellingham for a decade, so he must have been about 28 years old. Amanda had grown up in Spokane, and was trained in clas-sical cello. She seemed like a sweet, enthusiastic young woman. Amanda had an elaborate tattoo on her back just below her neckline. Her tattoo depicted a large romantic moon behind some tall trees.

Two more students sat in overstuffed furniture around a large table. They were Ashley Place and Peter Lee. Ashley grew up in a small town near Seattle. Peter was born in Bellingham, where he had lived most of his life. He seemed distracted and not very committed to the university. He threw out a somewhat snide comment about WWU students not being paid for their work as page turners. Dirk would have thought the college's mission was to provide learning experiences, not wages.

Dirk next met Wesley Walker, who said he grew up mostly in Colorado until his family moved to southern Oregon. Wesley said he had known Steve Ostrander well. They were roommates at a dorm as freshmen, and had shared an apartment as sophomores. They had found separate living quarters as juniors, but had remained close friends.

Steve's parents and sister had died in the crash of a small airplane, piloted by his father, when Steve was 16. He had lived with his grandparents in Utah until moving into a dorm at WWU. Although nominally a Mormon, Steve had become rather wild as a college student. As handsome as he was, and with his innate charm and his tragic back story, he was irresistible to women. Sometimes he tried to fend them off, and other times he submitted to their attentions and demands. Wesley recalled many nights when Wesley had to study late at the library or find something else to do because Steve needed privacy in their dorm room. Yet Steve never had a real girlfriend or any relationship that lasted more than a few weeks. Beneath his sunny disposition, Steve struggled with depression and survivor guilt stemming from the plane crash that he had escaped merely by not joining his parents and sisters for that particular trip. When women realized how suffocated by depression Steve was, they drifted away and he did not make any effort to hold onto them.

Even so, Dirk wondered, without saying anything to Wesley, whether one of the many girls who had shown an interest in Steve might have been jealous of the others. Another angle of inquiry might be the boyfriends of Steve's conquests.

"Do you know what Steve's class schedule was?" Dirk asked. Perhaps Dirk could contact some of Steve's classmates on campus and find out more about his relationships.

"I have an electronic copy of his schedule," Wesley replied. "I could email it to you. The cops already took his laptop."

Dirk wrote down his email address for Wesley.

Then he mingled for a bit, saying hello to several members of the musical society. One man was talking about his Mercedes collection. Apparently he owned four or five Mercedes. Another man said he wanted to buy a Mercedes that would be about 10 years old — affordable but not on the verge of falling apart.

"Just don't buy a diesel Mercedes," Dirk said.

"Why not?" asked the owner of the Mercedes collection.

"Because their exhaust stinks," Dirk declared. "A luxury car should not stink like a bus."

"My favorite is a diesel," said the collector. "It's the most comfortable of my cars and the most fun to drive. It also gets the best mileage."

Dirk thought to himself: Maybe I should have kept my mouth shut. But damn it, people who drive diesel cars need to hear the truth: Their cars stink.

Before leaving the reception, Dirk touched base with Mary Locke, the hostess. In a corner, away from the other guests, Dirk and Mary compared notes about Saundra Miller and Bliss. Saundra's story was that she had spent an hour with Steve at his apartment after the concert, and he had been fine when she left. It was still early enough when she left that he could have gone out again by himself, Saundra had told Mary.

Mary mentioned that she had tried to interest Saundra in attending an opera in Mount Vernon, about 30 minutes south of Bellingham, but Saundra had demurred.

"Apparently, string instrumentalists generally are not very interested in opera," Mary said. "They are so focused on their instruments that they overlook the vocal arts."

"Or maybe she just isn't interested in second-string opera companies in small cities," Dirk said.

Dirk now zeroed in toward Adrian Mondragon, owner of the motorcycle shop where the Miller/Bliss concert had been held, to ask some more questions. Dirk asked Mondragon why an untested student had served as page turner at the concert instead of old reliable Frank Speaker, the retired opera professor.

"Don't tell him I said this, but Frank is getting a little too feeble for this kind of work," Adrian commented. "But he does not want to admit it. He's been standoffish toward me ever since that concert."

On his way out, Dirk said hello to former Bellingham Mayor Howard Penthouse. Dirk and Penthouse often played handball. Penthouse was a fierce opponent on the indoor handball court.

"I hear the city is going to annex Yew Rock Mobile Home Park," Penthouse said. "Then you will have to follow some rules."

"You always say that, Howard. And it never happens."

"When are we going to play handball again?"

"When you learn how to play by the rules," Dirk teased his pal. "Give me a call."

Chapter 6

Mac Martino visited Dirk in the morning. Martino was a neighbor at Yew Rock Mobile Home Park. He often dropped by for coffee in the morning.

"I hear you're involved in a murder investigation," Mac remarked. "I hope you haven't lost your magic touch. The Sheriff's Department probably is not up to the job, in my opinion."

Mac bore a longstanding grudge against local government. He thought of himself as a recycling paragon, but city and county officials regarded him as a hoarder and a non-conformist gadfly, as in not conforming to local zoning and building codes. Before he moved to Yew Rock, public officials tried to force Mac to clean up his home and yard. Dirk found Mac's rebellious streak refreshing, and he admired the older man's dedication to helping other people, always in his own peculiar way.

Dirk said he wished he could meet some of Steve Ostrander's classmates. Mac suggested that Dirk recruit young Isaac Casey to attend Steve's classes and chat up the girls.

"He's a handsome kid," Mac declared. "Now with his hair shorter and his weight back up, he looks good. In my opinion he might have had lice when we met him."

Mac and Dirk had met Isaac once when the two older men had been lost in the woods south of Bellingham. Isaac knew where he was geographically but he did not know his place in society. He had been camping in the woods part-time and sleeping on the couches of friends part-time. After Isaac led Mac and Dirk out of the forest, Dirk invited Isaac to stay with him, in a spare bedroom, until he could find a job.

"He didn't have lice, but that's not a bad idea," Dirk responded to Mac's suggestion. "Isaac works nights at the restaurant, and Steve's classes are in the day, so Isaac probably could slip into those classes. The quarter just started so I doubt that the professors recognize the faces of all the students in their classes yet."

"Maybe Isaac even will get interested in going to college," Mac added.

Isaac had moved into an apartment in the York neighborhood of Bellingham. Dirk called him and invited him to lunch at a Thai restaurant near Isaac's apartment.

They shared an order of coconut soup plus pork and noodles. The manager, a thin and pale German immigrant, served them. The manager had married one of the daughters in the Thai family that owned the restaurant, which was not busy today. The manager asked Dirk whether Cuban music was OK. It was.

"I'm celebrating the end of the Cold War between Cuba and the United States," the manager declared.

"Maybe President Obama will win another Nobel Peace Prize," Dirk joked.

"Obama never deserved the Nobel Prize in the first place," Isaac protested. "Maybe he finally will do something spectacular in his last months in office in order to deserve the prize."

Dirk explained what he wanted Isaac to do, and the young man agreed without much hesitation.

"I owe you that much," Isaac conceded. "I will go to some of his classes. But I don't know what you think I'm going to find out, just by sitting in class. What if a professor takes roll?"

"You can say you hope to add the class if it's not full," Dirk said. "I just want you to listen to what the students are saying. I think some of the students will be talking about Steve. You could ask some questions. You could be the one person in class who does not know anything about Steve or what happened to him. Try to find out which students were friends of Steve — and which were not. Get their names if you can. I'll take it from there."

"It's just like old times," Isaac commented, "with you and Mac meddling in a police investigation."

"I'm going to write a magazine piece about this," Dirk said. "The police think people are meddling when sometimes we're just doing our jobs or being good citizens."

Mac later dropped by Dirk's home for an update. With assurances that Isaac was on board regarding the infiltration of Steve Ostrander's classes, Mac turned his attention to an arsenal of anti-mouse materiel on the counter of Dirk's kitchen.

"Do you have a problem with mice?" Mac asked.

"I think so," Dirk replied. "It started when I put out a bird feeder last winter. Everything was OK until spring, when I noticed a hole in a plastic bag of bird seed I was keeping in a closet. There were shells of sunflower seeds scattered near the bag, and I think a mouse was nibbling on the seeds."

"There are three ways to get rid of mice," Mac declared. "Poison works, but the sick mouse might crawl inside a wall and die, and you have to smell it for a few days. Mouse traps probably are more humane, at least when they kill instantaneously, but sometimes they only maim, and then you hear the poor little mouse screaming until you put it out of its misery. The third way is ultrasonic beepers to annoy and drive out the mice. I see you have opted for traps and ultrasound."

Dirk had purchased an armful of traps, plus four ultrasound beepers. The unopened packages sat on the counter.

"I was going to try both, but now that I know I might hear mice screaming in the middle of the night, I think I will forget the traps for now, and plug in the beepers."

"In my opinion you are a bit squeamish," Mac said.

"I don't like to kill other creatures, especially my fellow mammals," Dirk acknowledged.

"Perhaps you are afraid of death," Mac ventured.

"Indeed I am," Dirk confirmed. "I do not look forward to a universe without me in it."

"I've had a woodpecker pounding on my walls," Mac noted. "Apparently they can't tell the difference between real wood and vinyl, because vinyl sounds like hollow wood and woodpeckers are looking for wood hollowed out by insects, which the woodpeckers eat. But woodpeckers are not mammals so I guess you won't mind so much if I have to kill them."

"Ah, so we have winged rodents as well," Dirk sighed.

Richard Howland

Chapter 7

Dirk and Isaac met for lunch again a few days later at a Mexican restaurant.

"I wonder why we have so many Mexican restaurants in the United States, when I don't remember ever seeing a Spanish restaurant," Isaac remarked. "Mexico is closer than Spain."

Dirk pointed out that Spanish restaurants usually have the terms "tapas" or "bodega" in their names. Tapas is a Spanish style of appetizer, and bodega is Spanish for cellar, as in wine cellar.

At an adjacent table was a large family with newborn twins. Dirk and Isaac overheard someone say that the twins had been premature, but they were chubby and healthy now.

"Do you think they are boys or girls?" Isaac asked Dirk. "They look like their father so I hope they're boys."

"They're wearing pink so I hope they're girls," Dirk said.

After their food arrived, Isaac complained that it was too salty.

"Most customers like salty foods," Dirk noted.

"Are you defending the restaurants?" Isaac demanded huffily. "Salt is not healthy."

"I'm looking at it from their point of view," Dirk explained.

Changing the subject, Dirk asked: "What have you learned about Steve Ostrander?"

"Steve apparently was pretty close to a girl named Kay Day," Isaac reported. "She is studying classical guitar. You can see her yourself tomorrow because she will work with a visiting musician during a master class that will be open to the public.

"Another girl you might check out is Abigail Baker, who plays piano," Isaac continued. "I gathered that she knew Steve way back in grammar school — even kindergarten, maybe. But he apparently did not have time for her anymore, and he kept his distance. I got the impression that she adored him from afar. I doubt that the police even know about her because I do not think they were in email contact or were Face Book friends. She is really interested in local trees and wildlife as inspiration for her music. After I chatted with her, she invited me to go on a 'tree walk' Sunday. Some guy will lead a tour of the campus, identifying this and that tree. It's open to the public so you can go to that, too."

So Dirk went first to the master class, taught by Bill Saint James. In his 30s, Saint James was a handsome, slender man with curly black hair and an engaging smile. He wore an open-collar, dress white shirt, sport coat, designer jeans and loafers.

He looked like a GQ fashion model but did not appear to be the least bit conceited. He was personable and seemed genuinely interested in each of the four students with whom he worked, touching their hands, arms, shoulders and knees. Born in England and now a resident of New York City, Saint James spoke with an upper class accent as you might expect to hear from a member of the royal family.

The first student performed "Solearas" by Martin Escudero. After her recital, Saint James urged her to face the audience more directly in order to make a connection with the people out there.

"When you talk to someone, you don't look off to the side. So when you play music for someone, you should not look off to the side," Saint James instructed. "The audience wants to make a connection with you."

The next student performed "Asturias-Leyenda," originally composed for piano by Isaac Albeniz (1860-1909), a Spanish pianist and composer.

Saint James advised this young man to keep his wrist straight and to curve his fingers instead of his wrist. Like a tennis player, you should "play with your whole body, not just the wrists," Saint James advised.

"Pure movement is using the right muscle with the right amount of energy," he added. "Music is about creating three-dimensionality. Music is creating tension and releasing it."

The third student was Kay Day, the close friend

of Steve Ostrander. Saint James had reminded each of the students to straighten their backs in order to avoid back pain throughout their careers. He seemed particularly drawn to Kay, touching both of her shoulders in order to straighten her spine. Saint James also urged Kay to "feel the tension in the string, like an archer does. If an archer does not pull hard on the string, the arrow does not go far."

Kay was a short, pretty blonde with long hair down to the middle of her back, and her hair had been set in some kind of permanent so it formed a hypnotic curl or wave. Dirk pondered how he might approach her to talk about Steve. No suitable tactic materialized in his mind, and he left it for another day.

The final student was a young man. Saint James said the final student's technique was excellent but he needed to play with more passion.

"Rodin said, 'I am the landscape that I'm painting.' You must be the music you are playing," Saint James urged.

Saint James now welcomed questions from the audience. An old woman asked how often he tunes his guitar.

"There is an old joke about guitarists," Saint James replied. "Guitarists spend half their lives tuning their guitars and the other half playing out of tune."

Dirk wondered whether he would hear any tree jokes when Dirk and Isaac joined the tree tour on

Sunday at Western Washington University. About 30 people participated in the walk, which began at 2 p.m. at Red Square in a light rain. Abigail Baker arrived a little late and settled in next to Isaac, who did not introduce her to Dirk. That had been their plan.

The leader of the tour introduced himself to the group by saying he had earned a degree in literary history at WWU in 1976, with a minor in art history. During a 30-year career as a parks and recreation employee, he had become a self-taught expert on the trees of North America. He said there were about 160 species of trees on campus.

He started the tour by pointing out an abundance of London plane trees throughout Red Square. Plato had instructed his students under a plane tree, the tour leader said. Now about 70 percent of street trees in London, England, are plane trees. Since the 1600s they have stood up well to pollution and compacted soil. The London plane is an early hybrid of the American sycamore and the Oriental plane.

Also very common on campus were big-leaf maples.

"Maples are the swingers of the tree world," the tree expert said, "because they can reproduce among male and female trees, male and male trees or female and female trees."

So, today's tree joke was a "dirty" joke, Dirk thought.

Near the library but still adjacent to Red Square were several young river birch, which the tour leader said were gradually replacing the Himalayan white birch on campus, which were dying under assault by insects not found in the trees' native Nepal.

On the west side of the old library was a decade-old gum tree, which bees inexplicably loved, according to the tour leader. The group also studied a Chinese scholar tree. Supposedly the Chinese planted these trees at the graves of scholars, although the tour leader said they were more likely to grace the burial plots of important bureaucrats. Imported to Japan, it now is found near pagodas and sometimes is called the pagoda tree.

Walking toward Old Main, the group stopped in front of a burr oak. The leader said people on campus once thought this was a Washington state champion white oak. He said he never had seen acorns on the tree. Dirk picked up a small nut from the ground and asked whether it might be an acorn.

"Nice try," the leader responded. "But that's a beechnut from the beech behind the oak."

Next the group stopped at a black locust with invasive holly growing on it. Near the west entrance to old Wilson Library were some Lombardy poplars. The tree expert said farmers often planted these tall trees as windbreakers. They only lived to be about 100 years old. These poplars were planted in 1928, when Wilson Library was built.

Between the library and the student union was an American elm, believed to be resistant to Dutch elm disease, a blight that had not reached Whatcom County yet. In a small arboretum across High Street from the student union was a Pacific yew, rare now because poachers had cut down so many for production of a cancer treatment. Nearby was a Chinese ghost tree.

Then the group approached one of Dirk's favorite trees on campus: a huge old plane tree with ugly burls. This specimen, *pyramidalis*, was a larger mutant of the smaller London plane. The tour leader said this old plane tree was one of his favorites.

From there the group walked to another giant: a sequoia. The tree expert said it was the largest sequoia in Bellingham. The sequoia triggered memories for Abigail, who mentioned to Isaac that she had seen a woman being struck and killed by lightning at a rock outcrop in Sequoia National Park in California.

Nearby were a yellow buckeye, native to the eastern and southeastern United States, and a burning bush. Isaac said he liked the burning bush. Also nearby were a Norway maple Crimson King, a Persian ironwood, an Atlas cedar, a camperdown elm (which looked like a large mushroom) and a *Taiwania cryptomerioidius*, a coniferous tree in the cypress family. Most trees called cedars in North America actually are members of the cypress family, but the Atlas is a true cedar.

The hour-long tour ended there. The group was slightly smaller than it had been at first, but most of the people had remained interested throughout the tour, and now they expressed their appreciation to the leader. Isaac and Abigail walked away together. Dirk went home.

Dirk met Isaac for breakfast the next day.

"Abigail mentioned last night that when Steve was at Central Washington University, he got into some kind of fight with an autistic guy," Isaac reported. "Steve was involved in a demonstration against keeping chimpanzees on campus for research. The autistic guy worked for the chimpanzee research program, and he attacked Steve."

"What kind of research was going on?" Dirk asked.

"It had something to do with communication between humans and chimpanzees," Isaac answered. "The autistic guy apparently was very comfortable with the chimps — more comfortable than he was with people. So he felt threatened by the demonstrators who wanted to shut down the chimp program. Maybe this autistic guy followed Steve to Western Washington and attacked him again."

"Was Steve hurt badly at Central? Was the autistic guy punished?"

"No and no."

"If it was just a scuffle, it doesn't seem likely that this guy would travel across the mountains to stalk Steve. I wonder if an autistic person would even be capable of planning and carrying out an act of revenge."

"I don't know," Isaac said.

"It's worth looking into," Dirk concluded.

Dirk had been planning a road trip with his young daughter to Coulee Dam in Central Washington. Central Washington University was near coulee country, and a stop there to look into the chimpanzee program would fit right into his travel plans. His girl's mother and the girl lived in Olympia, and for the first five years of the girl's life, Dirk had not known the girl existed. Then the mother had reached out to Dirk, introduced him to his daughter, Ginny, and belatedly welcomed him into Ginny's life.

He went online and learned that the last two chimps at CWU were moved to a sanctuary in Quebec in 2013. Tatu and Loulis, who had learned American Sign Language and had interacted with human researchers at CWU, were integrated with 11 other chimpanzees at the 200-acre sanctuary in Quebec. Earlier two other chimps at CWU had died, and officials had decided the remaining pair needed social contact with a larger group of chimps. It would have been expensive to bring new chimps to CWU, so transferring Tatu and Loulis to a larger facility was the better option. The founders of the chimp program at CWU had retired. Prior to the closure of the chimp habitat, graduate students and undergraduates had participated in research at the CWU facility. Researchers had

sought the "consent" of the chimps for every project. If a chimp did not want to do something called
for in a particular project, the humans would
abandon the project, according to the Web site.

Dirk tried to find information about the assault
against Steve Ostrander. Ellensburg's newspaper, The Record, had nothing in its online archive
about an autistic young man attacking a demon-
strator, and nothing at all about Ostrander. Dirk
tried the Web site of Banks Library at CWU, but
he needed a student or faculty I.D. number in order to access the archives. Perhaps he would have
a better chance of success in person.

Chapter 8

Dirk and Ginny left Olympia at about 9 a.m. and drove east and then north on Interstate 5 to the city of Federal Way, between Tacoma and Seattle. Then they followed Highway 18 to Snoqualmie Falls, where they stopped for a break. Famous as a backdrop for a former TV series, "Twin Peaks," the 268-foot falls was an impressive sight despite the distraction of an ugly power plant near the top. Massive though it was, this hydroelectric plant generated just 1 percent of Puget Sound Energy's electricity. Ginny, now 7, had never seen such a big waterfall.

"Where does all of this water come from?" she asked.

"It comes from the snow on the nearby mountains," Dirk said. "The snow melts into water and the water trickles down here in creeks and streams."

They also stopped in the nearby town of Snoqualmie, where Ginny could see the snow on the mountains a little better. Dirk took some photos of Ginny standing amid several plum trees in pink bloom in front of an old wooden building that was painted yellow. They found a very modern city hall in the center of town. Then they drove a little farther south to Interstate 90, on which they crossed the Cascade Mountains to the east.

They ate lunch at a Mexican restaurant in Cle Elum on the other side of the mountains. The name of this town, incorporated in 1902, came from a Native American term for "swift water," in reference to the Cle Elum River. The town's population was about the same as its elevation in feet: 1,900. A local guidebook said Dick Scobee, commander of the ill-fated Challenger space shuttle, was born here.

As they entered, Dirk noticed a family that appeared to be praying at their table. The slender young father, the attractive mother and their daughter held their heads down. Dirk thought how nice it was that a family would feel comfortable praying at a public restaurant. You might not see that in a big city. Then he realized they were staring into their electronic devices, not praying.

Before leaving Cle Elum, they drove past the Carpenter House, which Dirk had discovered in a local guidebook from the Mexican restaurant. A banner in front of the house heralded the 100th anniversary of the house, built in 1914 by banker and mayor Frank Carpenter. His only living descendant donated the house to the Kittitas County Historical Society in 1989. The house was not open today but Dirk snapped a photo of its exterior. The streets near the house were very wide because the wife of the town founder anticipated that Cle Elum would become a great city, as the capital of a coal-producing region. She had been a little too optimistic.

Dirk and Ginny drove about 20 miles southeast to Ellensburg, where they checked into a Hampton Inn. Dirk was afraid that noise from the adjacent I-90 and a nearby truck stop would disturb their sleep, but the desk clerk assured him that "no one complains about freeway noise." Dirk had wondered, while making reservations online, why hotel rates tonight were higher than the day before and the day after, throughout Ellensburg, so he asked the clerk why this was. The clerk said there was a robotics competition at Central Washington University in Ellensburg, which had attracted a lot of students, teachers and parents.

Ellensburg, incorporated in 1883, was a city of less than 20,000 people. It was flat, with a lot of colorful brick buildings downtown. In the late 19th century, Ellensburg had vied to become the state capitol, but lost to Olympia. The surrounding dry fields now supported immense hay growing and processing operations. Dirk later read an article in the student newspaper at CWU, which said local hay growers had been hurt during a recent labor slowdown at West Coast ports. Growers had been unable to move their product to their overseas customers.

After checking into the hotel, Dirk and Ginny drove east on Vantage Highway to Gingko

Petrified Forest State Park. They could have taken I-90, which was parallel to Vantage Highway and a little bit south of Vantage Highway, but Dirk preferred a less stressful route. They passed Whiskey Dick Mountain (elevation 3,878 feet) and the Wild Horse Wind and Solar Facility, owned by Puget Sound Energy. As they approached the state park, the highway wound through Schnebly Coulee, Dirk and Ginny's first taste of many coulees to come. A coulee is a now dry channel formed long ago by a melting glacier.

It appeared to be the off-season for Gingko Petrified Forest State Park. Two college-age girls were leaving as Dirk and Ginny arrived, and a mixed-race (Asian and Caucasian) couple arrived just before they left. There were no other visitors. An interpretive center was closed, but a ranger who lived on site encouraged Dirk and Ginny to backtrack to the west entrance of the 7,470-acre park, where they could walk on the trails. He promised they would see wildflowers. First they checked out the petroglyphs on display outside the interpretative center, facing the Wanapum Reservoir on the Columbia River. A few petrified logs sat nearby.

The petroglyphs had been moved from the nearby river banks before these artifacts would be flooded when Wanapum Dam was completed in 1963. Wanapum means "river people." The Wanapum were friendly to the Americans in the Lewis and Clark expedition in 1805, according to the explorer's journals. A plaque near the petro glyphs said the meaning of the inscriptions had been lost to history, but Ginny and Dirk recognized stick-like images of people, deer and the sun. Dirk wondered why the petro glyphs were unprotected in any way from the elements and from vandals, but he supposed that was why a ranger lived at the site.

"I can draw better than this," Ginny declared.

"You can draw better than this on paper, with a pencil or a crayon," Dirk agreed. "But these drawings were made hundreds of years ago, when the people who lived here did not have paper, pencils or crayons. Do you think you could draw on hard rock by using another hard rock to scrape the surface?"

They drove west on Vantage Highway and left their car at the other park entrance, where there was another stone house for a ranger.

Between 17 and 12 million years ago, the climate here was much wetter, supporting a lush forest. Volcanic ash buried this portion of the forest. Minerals gradually replaced the organic material of the trees, creating petrified wood. At the end of the last ice age, huge floods exposed the petrified wood. Highway workers in 1927 noticed the petrified trunks of ancient trees. The 3224th Company of the Civilian Conservation Corps occupied Camp Gingko in 1936 and built trails, a water system and a caretaker's home. At the entrance to the trails there was a photo of a half-dozen young men, shirtless and sweaty, working with shovels and picks under a hot sun in 1936.

His visit here made Dirk feel a little better about human-caused global warming. No humans existed 12 million years ago, and it always had been unlikely that humans still would be here on Earth in another 12 million years, with or without global warming. This was just the natural order of an ever-changing planet. But having Ginny along reminded Dirk that her generation likely would face severe disruptions in their lives due to climate change.

Ginny and Dirk started to walk up a trail.

"I don't want to walk up," Ginny complained. "I'd rather walk down."

"If you walk downhill first, then you have to walk uphill later when you might be tired and thirsty," Dirk said. "It's better to walk uphill first and then downhill. Do the hard part first and then do the easy part."

They hiked along a trail that went past several tree trunks, still below ground level and visible through heavy iron grates. Signs identified the trees as maple, Douglas fir, spruce and walnut. Dirk and Ginny did not go far enough to see any elm or gingko. They also saw the wildflowers promised by the ranger: white phlox and yellow sunflower. The same mixed-race couple that had been at the east entrance now arrived at the west entrance.

Dirk drove back to Ellensburg and looked for

a restaurant. He parked and walked in the downtown area, with Ginny holding his hand. They passed a skate park on Second Avenue. They wandered past Bailey's Biblomania, where banners proclaimed a 2-for-1 sale, but they did not enter. They did not have time to browse for books. Dirk later checked the store's Web site, which said it had more than 100,000 books in stock. They also found the office of the Daily Record, and they went inside to buy today's newspaper for 75 cents.

They decided to eat dinner at Ellensburg Pasta Company on Main Street. Dirk ordered a Henry Weinhard orange cream soda for Ginny because she was thirsty and he was familiar with Weinhard beer, although he had not known the brewer made soft drinks, too. The waitress was a college student whose one-word response to nearly everything was: "Perfect!"

After dinner they walked at the campus of Central Washington University, which was aglow with the fading light of the sun. After photographing some impressive willow trees, they walked to the Japanese Garden, but it was closed. All along the sidewalks there were banners hanging from lamp posts, with photos of prominent CWU graduates, including admirals and mayors. Dirk was surprised by one poster lionizing a Starbucks attorney. Was being a Starbucks attorney such a great accomplishment? Perhaps only in Washington state. They continued walking in a loop, following signs that led them to the Chimpanzee and

Human Communication Institute. A large caged area remained, but the chimps clearly were gone, and the building now served as an annex to the athletics department.

Chapter 9

Looking out the hotel window toward the east, Dirk and Ginny witnessed a surreal sunrise behind windmills in the hills. When they went downstairs to the breakfast room, it was crowded with about 50 high school kids, mostly boys. They wore blue jackets indicating that they were participants in the robotics competition at CWU. Dirk asked an adult where they were from, and he said they were from Hillsboro, Ore.

After breakfast Dirk and Ginny rode an elevator with one of the boys, who was taller than Dirk. Ginny asked him what kind of robot he had built. He said the competition called for robots that could stack recycling bins. He added that he participated in robotic competitions two or three times a year. He got out of the elevator on the second floor. Dirk and Ginny continued to the third and top floor. Dirk had not heard these robotics kids during the night, so they must have been well chaperoned and well behaved.

Dirk figured he had until the noon check-out time at the hotel to get some research done on campus. He brought some paper and crayons to keep Ginny occupied, and they visited the office of the Central Sentinel, a campus newspaper that was not part of the Journalism Department but instead was owned by the student body association. Students who worked for the Sentinel did not earn academic credit. Dirk found a bearded young man alone in the office. Luckily this editor was an Ellensburg native and a fifth-year student at CWU, and he remembered a demonstration against the chimp program in 2012. He thumbed through some files in a squeaky cabinet and found some articles about the demonstration.

According to the first article, an autistic volunteer at the chimpanzee center had taken offense to the demonstration and had lunged at one of the demonstrators. The article identified the victim as Steve Ostrander and the assailant as Bobby Baldovino. Subsequent articles indicated that a university committee had investigated the incident and had not disciplined Baldovino. He was a high-performing autistic who managed to get along well with people most of the time, and the prospect of further violence was not likely, according to the committee.

Dirk looked up the Baldovino family in a dusty phone book laying on a cluttered desk. He was surprised to find a listing on Vantage Highway, where he and Ginny had been yesterday. The family apparently lived on a ranch to the east of Ellensburg. So after checking out of the hotel, Dirk and Ginny drove east again past familiar terrain.

They found the address easily and started up a gravel driveway. About halfway between the paved road and a gate, a young man was working with a noisy leaf blower. Dirk got out of the car to speak to the young man. Ginny followed.

"Why are you stalking me?" demanded the young man, who appeared to be mentally unbalanced or on paranoia-inducing drugs.

"We're not stalking you," Dirk said. "We're just tourists. We're looking for the Gingko Petrified Forest."

"Go back where you came from or I'm going to gay-bash you," the man said. He was about Dirk's height but weighed a little more and was more muscular, not to mention that he was younger than Dirk.

"Are you Bobby Baldovino?" Dirk asked.

"None of your business!"

"Come on Ginny. Let's go," Dirk said, grabbing her hand.

"Why is that man so mad at us?" Ginny asked.

"He's not really mad at us," Dirk answered. "He's mad at himself for being a failure in life, and he's mad at the world for not giving him a better life."

They continued east on Vantage Highway again, merging with Interstate 90 and going across the Columbia River, where I-90 turned north. Within a few miles of the bridge, they stopped at Wild Horses Monument. They had seen the horse sculptures from the freeway, but now they climbed a steep trail for a closer look. When they reached the top, Ginny fell in love with these life-sized yet perfectly safe horses. Spokane artist David Govedare had created 15 animals out of steel. The first horse was placed on the hilltop in 1989, the year of Washington state's centennial. By now the rusty sculptures had been heavily defaced by graffiti. Across the river they could see Gingko Petrified Forest, where Dirk and Ginny had been yesterday.

They continued northeast from Frenchman's Coulee and passed through the town of George. With only 500 people, the town was so small that Dirk did not bother to leave the freeway. He thought they could see the whole town from I-90. According to Wikipedia, George, Wash., was the only town in the country bearing the first and last names of a president. A pharmacist founded the town in the 1950s. Residents planted cherry trees, perhaps in honor of a president who supposedly cut down a cherry tree as a child, but also because cherries are grown in the region.

The next dusty town was Ephrata, whose high point in history occurred on Aug. 4, 1934, during the Great Depression. At a time when dust storms were raging across the Great Plains, corn fields were stunted by drought, and longshoremen in Seattle were in combat against strikebreakers and police, a beacon of hope drew 20,000 people to tiny Ephrata to hear President Franklin Roosevelt speak. The president extolled the benefits that would come from construction of the Grand Coulee Dam. Among the benefits were abundant irrigation water for farms, cheap electrical power and thousands of jobs created by the development of a huge new infrastructure.

Just outside of Ephrata was a town called Soap Lake, where Dirk and Ginny left Highway 28 and followed Highway 17 north to Lake Lenore Caves State Park. Floods carved out the caves from the basalt walls of the Lower Grand Coulee about 12,000 years ago. Dirk and Ginny climbed through a rubble of basalt rocks to get to one of the caves. The day was cool and cloudy, and Dirk would not have wanted to hike very far here on a hot summer day. The cave they reached was large but shallow.

"Did cavemen live here?" Ginny asked.

"The tour book says native Indians used these caves while hunting in this area," Dirk answered.

Next they stopped at Dry Falls State Park Visitor Center. Dry Falls once was "the world's greatest water fall" at 3.5 miles wide with a height of 350 feet, according to a plaque. At the end of the last ice age, more water passed over these cliffs than the amount of water now carried by all the rivers in the world, according to geologists. Since then, the water has returned to the Columbia River channel.

They were hungry so they drove north to Coulee City for lunch. Coulee City had about 500 residents. Dirk saw only two restaurants, across the street from each other, and he picked the one that had several cars parked in front of it. The other one had no cars. The apparently more popular eatery was Steamboat Rock Restaurant, which recently had celebrated its 40th anniversary, according to a banner on the wall. The restaurant appeared to be run by a husband who cooked and a wife who served the food and worked the cash register. Dirk asked her whether she was an owner.

"I'm the chief flunky," she replied. "I've worked here 41 years."

Dirk ordered two salmon burgers, which were made from frozen patties.

Several of the other customers greeted each other by name. One young man was trying to sell farm equipment to an older potato farmer.

After lunch they drove north on Highway 155 to Steamboat Rock State Park, which was on a peninsula jutting into Banks Lake. The water in Banks Lake is pumped from nearby Roosevelt Lake, which itself was created by the Grand Coulee Dam on the Columbia River. It looked as though Steamboat Rock State Park would be very busy in the summer. There was a huge parking lot, a boat launch ramp, a playground, a swimming beach and campsites. A basalt butte called Steamboat Rock dominated the landscape.

Finally they drove north to a cluster of small cities surrounding Grand Coulee Dam. The City of Grand Coulee was above the dam. Electric City was to the west. The City of Coulee Dam was below the dam, where it straddled both sides of the

Columbia River. Elmer City was to the northeast. Why not have just one city? Perhaps the answer was that the dam itself lay within three counties: Okanogan, Douglas and Grant counties.

Dirk had made reservations at a motel in the City of Coulee Dam. While driving through the City of Grand Coulee on the way to Coulee Dam, Dirk spotted a Safeway market. He needed some carbonated water for indigestion, so he stopped at the Safeway. It took awhile to find carbonated water, and then they had to look for the candy aisle because Ginny wanted chocolate.

Dirk noticed a boy, who was about Ginny's age, sitting in a shopping cart as the boy's mother wheeled through the produce section. Kids at the supermarket often were engaged in their surroundings, learning the names of fruits and vegetables, learning how to shop, connecting with other shoppers through eye contact. This boy's face was buried in a small screen as he played some kind of electronic game. Dirk thought it was rather sad. The boy might as well have been in a bubble, isolated from human society.

Dirk and Ginny had to wait in a long line. It was a Friday afternoon and the store was very busy. Only three cash registers were open. Two more registers finally opened, but shoppers behind Dirk raced to those registers and he was stuck waiting where he was. Finally a store manager, who was a portly guy in his 50s, rang up Dirk's order. He asked whether Dirk had a Safeway Club

Card, and Dirk gave him his phone number. The manager recognized Dirk's area code so he knew that Dirk lived west of the Cascade Mountains.

"You have a $15 minimum wage there," he remarked.

"That's only in Seattle," Dirk said. "I live in Bellingham. But we do have a law in Bellingham banning plastic bags, so I'm in the habit of bringing my own canvas bags."

As Dirk handed the manager his bag, he realized that business people in the small towns of eastern Washington probably thought $15 an hour was a princely sum, considering that the cost of living surely was substantially lower in these small towns compared to Seattle. Perhaps it would be best to let each city or region determine its minimum wage, rather than having the state do it. Dirk wondered how much this Safeway was paying the high school kid who was bagging groceries. He was slender with a cocky smile and a mop of black hair. Another young man, blond and more muscular, was working the adjacent cash register, and probably earned more per hour.

Throughout this region Dirk had the feeling that people here were considerably different from people in western Washington, in lifestyle and attitude. Yet, although they might have felt distant from Seattle, geographically and culturally, people here apparently were rabid fans of the Seattle Seahawks football team, judging from the abundance of flags carrying the numeral "12" — a reference to the fierce fans who supplemented the 11 men on the field during Seahawks games by shouting and screaming their support strongly enough to constitute a "12th player."

Dirk quickly found the motel in the next city. The office was full of decorative bird houses, and Ginny hugged a cat that was lounging there. Dirk told the desk clerk that it seemed strange to see a cat amid all of those birdhouses. The clerk, a pleasant woman in her 40s, insisted that the cat was not the least interested in birds. Dirk and Ginny saw more birdhouses on the steep slope behind the inn, as they climbed the stairs to their room. The room was tiny, but people had complained online about the only other motel in town, which they said had even smaller rooms.

From a balcony they had a decent view of Grand Coulee Dam, but Dirk could not have said it was a pretty view. It had more of an industrial look. The massive dam was constructed between 1933 and 1942, during the Great Depression. It now was the largest electric power facility in the United States. Frank Banks, probably no relation to Dirk's friend Red Banks, was the chief construction engineer, and nearby Banks Lake was named for him. President Franklin Roosevelt visited the site and gave a rousing speech to dam workers in 1934. Seventy-seven workers died during construction. The dam was a severe blow to Native Americans, whose traditional hunting grounds were flooded and who lost access to salmon because the dam provided no fish ladders. The original purpose of the dam was to provide irrigation water, but during World War II the priority was to provide electricity to aircraft plants in Seattle, shipyards in Portland and plutonium production for atomic bombs at Hanford.

After he and Ginny had settled into the motel room, Dirk called Lt. Davis in Bellingham and told him about Bobby Baldovino in Ellensburg.

Davis was skeptical that an autistic young man would find his way across the mountains to stalk Steve Ostrander.

"Does he even have a driver's license?" Davis asked.

"That's the kind of thing you can find out a lot easier than I can. You're the investigator," Dirk said, while trying not to sound too sarcastic.

"I'll look into it," Davis said, as if maybe he would and maybe he wouldn't.

Dirk had asked the desk clerk to recommend a restaurant, and she had suggested Melody Restaurant, which was directly across the river from the inn. Dirk found it easily. It was in a strange building that looked like a bunker, perhaps a reflection of the nearby dam's design. Within this building was a bowling alley in addition to the restaurant.

Later online Dirk found a newspaper article about Melody Restaurant, which had been closed for 14 months until a new owner reopened it in 2013. The city provided a new walk-in refrigerator for the restaurant, and the mayor helped to re-paint it. The owner's background included restaurant experience in Los Angeles and Boise.

Dirk ordered a veggie wrap. Ginny had fish and chips. The waitress appeared to be Hispanic. While he waited for their food, Dirk watched a family at a nearby table. The father was in his late 40s or early 50s. His son probably was 16 or 17 and was overweight, perhaps a football player for his high school. The daughter was 12 or 13, and she was immersed in head phones, completely ignoring her family while the son bantered jocularly with his father, even taking a sip of his dad's beer. The mother was of a dark complexion, perhaps Native American or Romanian.

After they ate, Dirk and Ginny walked to a strip of grass, along Roosevelt Way, which served as a small park with a view of the dam. Here they sat for awhile.

When they returned to the restaurant parking lot, Dirk saw the boy who had been eating with his parents and his sister. He was driving away alone in a nice sports car.

Dirk and Ginny slept well. They ate breakfast at R&A Cafe, which offered "the best dam food in town," pun intentional. The cafe was around the block from Melody Restaurant and across Birch Street from Coulee Dam Casino, which was operated by the Coleville Confederated Tribes. They ordered veggie omelets. As they ate, the waitress chatted with a cop who was having breakfast. The cop sat at a rear booth, facing the door with his back to the wall. He wore a bulky, bullet-resistant vest. The waitress told the cop that she was planning a trip to Coeur d'Alene, Idaho, for her wedding anniversary. The cop said his anniversary was the same date as his in-laws' anniversary, and every year he forgot both anniversaries. Dirk struggled to determine what kind of cop he was. Finally he was able to read the officer's jacket: "Police Natural Resources Enforcement." Apparently he worked for the Washington Department of Natural Resources.

Dirk and Ginny left Coulee Dam at about 8 a.m. This time, instead of going south from Coulee City to Ellensburg, they continued west on Highway 2 toward Wenatchee. They passed through Moses Coulee, which in wet weather would collect rainwater and direct it into the Columbia River south of Wenatchee.

"Do you remember what a coulee is?" Dirk asked Ginny.

"Yes, it's where an old glacier melted," Ginny replied.

"Very good," Dirk said.

West of a small town called Waterville they began to see the first wild-growing trees they had seen up close since leaving the Cascade Range on their way east. They drove through Pine Canyon, which descended to the Columbia River, where Highway 2 hugged the bottom of the river gorge. They passed a lot of small apple orchards alongside Lake Entiat, a reservoir created in 1962 behind Rocky Reach Dam.

They crossed the river and drove through the northern outskirts of Wenatchee, continuing west on Highway 2 into the mountains, stopping in Leavenworth for lunch at Baren Haus. Leavenworth, a town of about 2,000 people, had transformed itself in the 1960s from a declining timber community into a booming Bavarian-style tourist magnet, inspired by the mock Danish town of Solvang in California. The sidewalks already were crowded with tourists, probably from Seattle, but no other customers were in the restaurant when Dirk and Ginny entered. But it was only 11 a.m. so Dirk figured the tourists were not hungry yet. Baren Haus made its own sauces and dough. The restaurant was in an old brick building with wooden floors. They sat next to the front window — a good spot for people-watching. Most of the tourists were in family groups, plus a few groups of college-age kids. Ginny had half of a Reuben sandwich. Dirk ate the other half, plus a schnitzel sandwich.

After lunch they stopped briefly at Wenatchee Lake. Continuing west, they encountered snow on the ground between Mill Creek Snow Park and Stevens Pass (elevation 4,061 feet). On the side of the road to Dirk's left near Gold Bar was a huge mass of apples. Apparently a truck carrying apples had spilled its load.

Richard Howland

Chapter 10

Dirk's neighbor, Mac Martino, dropped by in the morning for coffee. Dirk and Ginny were working on a scrapbook in which they were assembling mementos of their trip, such as business cards from restaurants where they ate and hotels where they stayed, newspaper articles about towns they visited, receipts, brochures and postcards. For Dirk, gathering and displaying souvenirs was a way of nourishing the afterglow of a good vacation, and he wanted the scrapbook to reinforce Ginny's memory of the trip.

After all, as the Roman emperor Marcus Aurelius said, "nowhere is there a more idyllic spot, a vacation home more private and peaceful, than in one's own mind, especially when it is furnished" with well preserved and pleasing memories.

While Ginny continued to add items to the scrapbook, Mac told Dirk that Mac was trying to persuade a friend to move to Yew Rock Mobile Home Park. A developer was trying to buy the friend's property in order to build a residential tower for low-income senior citizens. It would be the second phase of a two-tower project, adjacent to a tower that had been completed several years ago. During the permit process for the first tower, Mac's friend had opposed the project but the Bellingham City Council had approved it anyway. Now the friend still was resisting the developer's overtures.

Dirk recalled the story from his days as a reporter for the Bellingham Bugle. Mac's friend had rigged the roof of her building to create an exercise space for her disabled son. On days when it was not raining, the adult son had used a wheelchair to move around the roof, from exercise station to exercise station. The ground floor of the building contained retail and office space. Mac's friend and her son occupied an apartment on the second floor.

Now the friend was becoming infirm. Soon she would be unable to take care of her son, Mac said. Mac wanted her to sell her building to the developer, and move to a mobile home at Yew Rock.

"I could set up an exercise course for her son here at the park," Mac proposed. "Any residents here could use it. That would be a great amenity for the park, in my opinion. I can get the equipment we need. It won't cost you anything, Dirk."

"Sure, we could do that," Dirk said.

Mac wanted Dirk to meet his friend. Dirk agreed to go with Mac tomorrow, after returning Ginny to her mother tonight.

Mac and Dirk visited Mac's friend, Helen Alexander, the next day. Helen was a tall woman, taller than 6 feet, who had played basketball for the women's team at the University of Washington decades ago, going all the way back to the mid-1970s when the women's basketball program was new at UW. She towered over Dirk, who was 5-foot-8, and Mac, who was closer to 5-foot-7. Her height was one reason why she thought she would not fit into a mobile home.

"I keep telling her that mobile homes these days are not small," Mac said. He added to Helen, "You should see Dirk's home. It has Cathedral-style ceilings and windows. It's a great home, in my opinion."

"Fess Parker lived in a mobile home for a while," Dirk said. "And he was a tall man."

"I remember him from 'Daniel Boone' on TV," Helen noted. "But you're too young to be a 'Daniel Boone' fan."

"My father knew Fess," Dirk explained. "Fess and my father both were in the business of mobile home parks. Fess was the only man I've ever met who didn't look ridiculous while driving a Hummer, because he was so big. And he wasn't pretentious at all."

Helen led Mac and Dirk upstairs to the roof, where they met her son Johnny and they checked out the exercise stations.

"We could duplicate this on an even bigger scale at Yew Rock," Mac said with all the spit and polish of a politician making a campaign promise. "We even could find room for you to park a Hummer, if you want to get one."

Helen said she would think it over.

"Johnny always has dreamed of living on a boat, but I really could not fit in any boat small enough for me to afford," Helen noted.

"Why don't Dirk and I take Johnny down to the docks so he can see what living on a boat would be like?" Mac asked.

"That would be great," Helen said.

Mac just can't avoid getting ever more involved in peoples' lives, Dirk thought.

"Dirk, we can show him your dad's yacht," Mac added.

Mac scheduled a time and promised to pick up Johnny.

Mac was a compulsive good Samaritan. For example, he had been instrumental in arranging for residents of a rehabilitation home for alcoholic women to attend a weekly crafts class at Yew Rock Mobile Home Park. The older residents at the park showed the recovering alcoholics how to thread needles for sewing and how to create decorative gift boxes by molding paper around a block of wood. Some of the residents became mentors and substitute grandmothers to the alcoholics, demonstrating how to live fulfilling, sober lives. In exchange, the alcoholics gave the park residents much-needed attention as well as hugs and kisses.

With a new commitment signed and sealed to take Johnny to the docks, Dirk refocused on the Ostrander case. He met Isaac for dinner and for an update on whatever Isaac might have gleaned from Abigail.

A family entered the restaurant shortly after Dirk and Isaac sat down. The father was a bland, balding man in his 40s, and the mother was a nondescript woman. Their attractive two sons were the best showcase for the family genes that anyone could expect. One was about 22 and the other was about 20. All of the men in this family had hairy necks and arms. The younger son already was going bald.

Next, a pair of young brothers entered. One was about 16, short, well built and self-confident. The other was about 14, tall and slender, with a cute face and a shy demeanor. They seemed to be close friends as well as brothers. The older one seemed protective of the younger one.

Isaac reported that he and Abigail finally had talked forthrightly about her late friend, Steve Ostrander. Abigail had monitored Steve's snowballing binge drinking for months. The young man frequently drank himself into a stupor at parties. Then he would try to walk off the intoxication outdoors in the fresh air. Abigail sometimes followed Steve, trying to keep him out of trouble. His favorite place to walk was far from the campus, around the marina to Zuanich Park, which was on a manmade peninsula jutting into Bellingham Bay.

In his sober moments, Steve had taken up an extreme sport known as slack-lining, a category of tightrope walking. Isaac explained that a slack line was more flexible than a high wire or tightrope commonly used by circus acrobats. Practitioners walked on a slack line of considerable length and at considerable height outdoors, usually between tall buildings or across a gorge.

"It sounds like Steve was an adrenaline junk-ie," Dirk told Isaac. "He liked to push himself to the limit, by drinking himself into oblivion or risking life and limb on a tightrope."

Dirk believed this insight was worth communicating to Lt. Davis.

Chapter 11

Dirk called Lt. Davis in the morning. The lieutenant seemed to appreciate the tip about Steve Ostrander's habit of walking at the marina while drunk.

"Ostrander's clothing was soaking wet from rain when the body was found," Davis said. "But we found salt in the clothing, too. Someone might have hit him in the head at the Bellingham marina and fished him out of the water in order to move him to Birch Bay.

"That's off the record," the lieutenant added.

"I still think some of those motorcyclists at the recital might be involved in this," Dirk declared. "Ostrander might have gone out drinking with them."

"None of the bartenders we have interviewed can link him with the motorcycle bad boys," Davis said. "Like I told you before, they're accountants and lawyers. By the way, Baldovino's sister got a traffic ticket in Bellingham the morning after Ostrander died."

"Hey, then that was a solid lead I gave you," Dirk exclaimed.

"I have a friend at the Ellensburg Police Department. He's going to interview the Baldovino family. We need to find out what Bobby's sister was doing here, and whether Bobby was with him."

"I hope the Ellensburg cops don't shoot Bobby. He's not emotionally stable."

"When did you become a cop-hater?"

"I'm just yanking your chain. What about the sky-walking angle?" Dirk asked.

"There's no place to sky walk in Bellingham Bay."

"What if Steve fell from a slack line and died somewhere else, and his buddies dumped his body at Birch Bay because they did not want to get into trouble?"

"I don't know...," the lieutenant said, his voice trailing.

Dirk and Mac began to look into the slack-lining culture. Dirk found an announcement on line that a student from the University of British Columbia would attempt a crossing of the gorge the next day at Brandywine Falls, an hour or two north of Vancouver, B.C. Dirk and Mac decided to watch the attempt.

They left Yew Rock Mobile Home Park at 7:45 a.m. and drove north on Guide Meridian. They arrived at the Lynden border crossing about 10 minutes before it would open at 8. A semi-trailer truck and about 10 cars already were in line ahead. Only one lane opened at 8. The Canadian Customs building was under construction, and the border guard was on the right as Dirk and Mac approached him. Usually the border guards were on the left and they spoke primarily to the driver, but today the guard spoke to the passenger. Mac was driving Dirk's Forrester and Dirk was in the front passenger seat. The guard was a pleasant-looking young man with prematurely gray sideburns.

Dirk told him that he and Mac were going to Whistler for one night, and the guard asked where they planned to stay.

"At the Hilton," Dirk answered.

"How do you know each other?"

"We're neighbors."

They had waited about 40 minutes at the border. Now they continued north on Highway 13 but turned right on 8th Avenue so they could use a restroom at Aldergrove Regional Park. After leaving the restroom, Dirk and Mac saw a young woman pushing her beat-up Subaru, trying to start the engine by releasing the clutch while the vehicle was in motion. The two men helped her by pushing from the rear of the car so she could sit in the driver's seat and release the clutch. The car started with a sputter, and she drove away.

"Maybe she's going to Maine," Mac said.

"Why Maine?" Dirk asked.

"People go to Maine to hide. I've known four or five people who have moved to Maine after suffering some setback in life."

"Well, this is Canada so maybe she's going to New Brunswick."

Aldergrove looked like a nice place to hike, and Dirk thought he might return some day to spend more time there. But today they quickly resumed their journey north on Highway 13 and then west on Highway 1 to Mann Bridge, which crossed the Fraser River. Dirk was driving now, and he knew that Mann Bridge was a toll bridge, but he did not know how to pay the toll. He saw signs indicating an exit for motorists who wanted to pay the toll in cash, so he took the exit.

A clerk from India recorded Dirk's license number and discovered that Dirk had crossed the bridge a year ago without paying. Dirk told him that the bridge had been under construction at that time and Dirk had not realized that tolls were being collected. The clerk noted that the bridge still was under construction but tolls had been required for a long time. So Dirk had to pay for last year's crossing as well as today's. The clerk persuaded Dirk to register with the toll authority so he could receive a windshield sticker for electronic scanning, and whenever he crossed the bridge he would be billed.

Dirk and Mac continued on Highway 1 through Burnaby, North Vancouver and West Vancouver until they headed north on Highway 99, also known as the Sea-to-Sky Highway. With the traffic congestion of Vancouver behind them, they began to relax along the scenic road, which followed Howe Sound north toward Whistler. Howe Sound, a network of saltwater fjords, offered the tourist several provincial parks featuring green coves, intimate freshwater lakes and towering waterfalls.

Their first sightseeing stop was at Shannon Falls Provincial Park. A tour bus pulled into the parking lot shortly after Dirk parked, so he and Mac had to compete with a bunch of European tourists from the bus for vantage points. At 1,099 feet, the falls here were the third highest in British Columbia. (The tallest falls were on Vancouver Island.) Shannon Falls did not look like a good place to try a slack line. The rock walls were too high.

Dirk noticed the stumps of large trees, left behind when the area was logged about 90 years ago. In 1792, the explorer Capt. George Vancouver and his party camped near here. A guy named Shannon made bricks from the clay deposits in the 1890s. He sold the land to Brittania Copper Mines in 1900. A brewery bought the site in 1976, and donated the land to B.C. Parks in 1982.

When Dirk and Mac left Shannon Falls, they followed five Porsches out of the parking lot. There were three red Porsches, one white one and a silver one. The last of the five had an Ontario license plate. It was far from home.

Next they stopped at Stawamus Chief Provincial Park. They parked the car on the east side of Highway 99 and walked across a pedestrian bridge to the west side, but the view was obscured by trees and boulders. According to a sign, hiking in the park would be interrupted June 25-

26 and June 29-30 for filming a Paramount feature film titled "Washington."

They entered the town of Squamish shortly before noon, and they looked for an eatery called Naked Lunch, which Dirk had discovered online while researching and planning the trip. The eatery was supposed to be at the corner of Pemberton Avenue and 3rd Avenue, but they saw no restaurant there. They parked on the street in the shade of a large tree, and Mac asked a passerby where Naked Lunch was. The passerby had a shaved head and a stern face, but he spoke in a soft, friendly voice. He pointed to a shopping center northeast of the intersection, and said Naked Lunch was next to the Safeway Market.

They found the eatery. It was the kind of place where you submitted your order at the cash register and a server brought the food to your table. Dirk and Mac each had a grilled vegetable Panini and an Odwalla Mango Tango smoothie.

With about 17,000 residents, Squamish was at the far north end of Howe Sound, beyond which were the Coastal Mountains. Lorne Cardinal, a First Nation actor on the quirky Canadian TV series "Gas Station," lived in Squamish, according to Wikipedia. Dirk had watched the show in Bellingham on a Canadian station. A Western Forrest Products pulp mill at Squamish closed in 2006, leaving the town to rely on tourism and outdoor recreation as the basis of its economy. An article in the current edition of a free biweekly newspaper quoted an analysis by Squamish Savings, which found that the town had "an alarming poverty problem that is in contrast to our image as a young, hip and active community. This problem is getting worse." Residents had trouble finding jobs and affordable homes, the article added. Other analysts were more optimistic. Squamish was making the transition from an industrial to a post-industrial economy faster than most towns facing this problem, they said. The new Sea to Sky Gondola was attracting tourists and investment. Squamish was half-way between two "world-class destinations" — Vancouver and Whistler.

Dirk had not forgotten the motorcyclist who wore an orange shirt from a Squamish motorcycle shop during the concert at Mondragon Motorcycles in Bellingham. Lt. Davis had shown little interest in this motorcyclist. Just for the hell of it, Dirk stopped at the motorcycle shop and bought an orange T-shirt for himself.

After leaving Squamish they stopped at Alice Lake Provincial Park, and they walked around the small lake. There were several swimming beaches. Farther north they stopped at Brandywine Falls, where a daredevil had just begun to walk across a slack line from one side of the canyon to the other side, very close to the 230-foot waterfall. Among a small crowd of onlookers, men and women were taking many photographs, and Dirk joined them. The aerialist was barefoot and shirtless, wearing only short pants and a baseball cap, plus a safety harness attached to his waist and to the slack line. In his late 20s, he carried nary an ounce of surplus fat that might throw off his balance. He made it across without falling even once. A guy with a video camera taped an interview with the aerialist. During his research Dirk had found a Web site for Slack Life BC, and he wondered whether this interview might be posted to the Web site.

Dirk and Mac spent about 30 minutes chatting with the daredevil's associates. They learned that in slack-lining, the aerialist uses nylon webbing, which is not as rigid as wire or rope. The amount of tension can be adjusted. Wherever they walk, the slack line usually is tied to a tree on either side. Hobbyists often cross a slack line while barefoot in order to grip the line between the toes. They might use a pole or umbrella for balance, or they might walk freehanded. Most sky walkers wear a harness attached to the main line to catch them if they lose their balance.

Dirk wondered whether slack-lining was legal, and the friends of the daredevil insisted that it was.

"We follow sensible safety precautions and we don't damage the environment," one said.

"What about the trees?" Dirk asked.

"We don't use trees with a diameter of less than 30 centimeters," said one enthusiast. "We're careful not to damage the tree. We cushion the strap with towels or carpet or maybe cardboard."

According to these enthusiasts, hot spots of interest in the sport included the University of British Columbia in Vancouver and Evergreen State College in Olympia, Wash.. There also was a club at Western Washington University in Bellingham. Indeed, while walking at WWU, Dirk had seen students practicing their skills on a slack line stretched between two trees just a foot or two above the ground. He also had seen them walking across a whirlpool fed by the creek that winds through Whatcom Falls Park in Bellingham. The whirlpool crossing surely was not for beginners.

The young people to whom Dirk and Mac talked were aghast at the very idea that slack-liners might try to cover up an accident. Despite the questionable legality of their art, they would certainly summon law enforcement in case of injury or death, they insisted. No one at Brandywine Falls admitted to knowing anything about Steve Ostrander, but Dirk thought he saw a flicker of recognition in the face of one young man. This youth drifted away from the group, and Dirk asked a young woman who this young man was. She said he was an American, but not from Washington. His name was Marcus Perfecto-Gomez, from Oregon. Dirk wrote down the name.

In the car, as they resumed their journey north, Mac said he and Dirk could recruit their young friend Isaac to join the slack-lining club at Western Washington.

"It probably would take him too much time to learn the sport before meeting enough people to make it worthwhile," Dirk demurred.

Dirk and Mac soon entered Whistler, which had hosted the 2010 Winter Olympics. Although better known as a winter ski resort now, Whistler started as a summer resort in 1914 with the opening of the Rainbow Lodge. Skiing began in 1966. They checked into a Hilton Hotel. In the lobby Dirk grabbed a free copy of the National Post, printed in Toronto. Reading it later, he was struck by how right-wing the National Post's editorial pages seemed, despite Canada's reputation as a left-leaning nation. Parking at the hotel was $30 per day, compared to $10 per day at the nearby convention center. So Dirk and Mac took their luggage to their rooms on the seventh floor and then returned to the lobby to park the car at the center. One of three or four doormen on duty had taken Dirk's car keys, and Dirk gave him a Canadian $2 coin as a tip when he retrieved the keys.

"Thanks, mate," he said. Dirk thought the doorman's accent was Australian. Many of the hotel staff members seemed to be Australian, perhaps because it was winter in Australia when it was summer in Canada, and because both countries were part of the British Commonwealth.

Dirk and Mac drove to the convention center and parked the car. Then they walked along The Village Stroll, a pedestrian mall with Whistler Olympic Plaza at the north end and Mountain

Square and Skiers Plaza at the south end. Shops, galleries and restaurants lined the wide, zigzagging pathway. Among the ambling tourists were two chubby white men in their 30s or 40s walking with three young boys — two black and one white.

Dirk thought about calling Lt. Davis to tell him about Marcus Perfecto-Gomez, the guy at Brandywine Falls who claimed to know nothing about Steven Ostrander, but Dirk did not have anything more than a hint of a hunch. It could wait. Dirk did not want to make an international call, anyway.

Dirk and Mac ate dinner at the BG (Bread Garden) Urban Grill. Most of the customers were sitting outside in the sun, but Mac wanted to sit inside, out of the sun. The host took them to a small table near an open door, where they felt a cool breeze. An overhead television was showing a baseball game featuring the Toronto Blue Jays vs. the New York Mets. Rap music blared over the sound system, and Mac said maybe they had made a mistake in selecting a restaurant with the word "urban" in the name. But later the restaurant played some disco music by Diana Ross and Donna Summers, reflecting more eclectic tastes in music. The waiter, when he appeared, smelled of cologne. Mac ordered spaghetti with meatballs. Dirk ordered a Tuscan Veggie and a tropical fruit salad.

Mac and Dirk left Whistler at 9:30 a.m. the next day. About halfway between Whistler and Squamish they spotted a unique mountain, which

Dirk later learned was called The Black Tusk. Aptly named, it had the shape of a sharp tooth or horn, thrust into the air. Wikipedia described it as the remnant of an extinct strato-volcano, or "a pinnacle of volcanic rock," soaring 7,600 feet above sea level. The Squamish Tribe called it "the landing place of the thunderbird." Dirk and Mac looked for somewhere along the highway to stop and take a photo of The Black Tusk. When they finally did stop, there were power lines between them and the peak, but Dirk took a photo anyway. Those power lines had dogged them all the way to Whistler and back, and it had been a difficult task to keep them out of the photos that Dirk took.

Again they ate at Naked Lunch in Squamish. After lunch, their next stop was Porteau Cove Provincial Marine Park, which had a beach and a pier offering expansive views of Howe Sound. The pier served as an emergency ferry terminal in case a rock slide or avalanche closed Highway 99.

They drove into Vancouver, stopping at Stanley Park where they napped for 20 minutes at Third Beach. Then they walked to Siwash Rock and back to Third Beach. They drove to Second Beach and strolled some more. The beaches were crowded, and Dirk wondered why so many people were not at work. Perhaps they worked at night. Dirk had paid $6 for two hours of parking at Stanley Park, and when their parking permit expired they drove through downtown Vancouver toward Richmond. Traffic was very congested on Oak Street.

By the time they made it to Richmond they were tired of fighting traffic so they stopped at the first retail center they saw, and they found a restaurant where they could eat slowly and wait for traffic to lighten a little. They selected a Boston Pizza, part of a chain with 350 restaurants in Canada. It was a sports bar with big TV screens perched seemingly in every nook and cranny. There was fake wrestling on the screens nearest to Dirk's table. Much as he tried, he could not avoid watching the clownish wrestlers. The camera angle changed every couple of seconds, commanding Dirk's brain to pay attention. He felt like he had little control over his brain.

They decided to see the Richmond Library in order to kill more time and let traffic dissipate. Dirk asked their server, a pleasant young woman in her early 20s, where Richmond's library was, and she gave directions. Dirk and Mac found the library easily. It was after 6 p.m. by now, and Dirk was afraid the library might be closed. Bellingham's library usually closed at 6, but Dirk figured that Richmond, with so many education-focused Asian residents, would keep its library open later. Indeed, the hours were 9 a.m. to 9:30 p.m. Monday through Friday and 10 a.m. to 5 p.m. Saturday and Sunday. That was better than Bellingham Library's hours.

After they left the library, traffic was light through the oft-congested Massey Tunnel under the Fraser River. Dirk and Mac could see Sisters,

Mount Baker and Mount Shuksan from the highway, and they spotted three hang gliders hovering near the highway.

There was only one car ahead of them at the border. The guard was Asian, and he spoke with an accent, probably a Cantonese accent. He asked only a few questions before waving them through.

Chapter 12

The next day, Dirk and Mac took Johnny, their prospective new tenant at Yew Rock Mobile Home Park, to the marina at Squalicum Harbor. Johnny's mother did not go, but Mac and Dirk borrowed her van, which was equipped with a wheelchair ramp.

The three men strolled along the trail around the marina, with Dirk and Mac taking turns pushing Johnny's wheelchair, in order to give Johnny an overview of the marina, operated by the Port of Bellingham since 1922.

Dirk did not want to bore Johnny with a dry history of the waterfront, but he reminded himself that recorded history at Bellingham Bay began in the 1790s, when two European expeditions visited. The first was commanded by the Spanish explorer Francisco Eliza. The second was under the command of Lt. Joseph Whidbey of England, who sailed into Bellingham Bay in a small boat attached to a larger expedition led by Capt. George Vancouver.

England and the United States both claimed the territory until agreeing in 1846 to draw a boundary along the 49th parallel, and Bellingham Bay, named for an associate of Capt. Vancouver, became part of the United States. In 1853 two pioneers named Roeder and Peabody built a timber mill at Whatcom Creek. Roeder found coal (or "black fire dirt," as the native people called it). He sold the coal rights to a guy named Cornwall. The only way to reach Bellingham was by boat until 1921, when Chuckanut Drive, a scenic coastal road, opened to automobiles.

It was a beautiful, warm day. Four shirtless fishermen were working on a boat. Most of them were old guys with deeply wrinkled skin. Judging from their dark complexions and their round faces, they probably were local Lummi Indians. But one was a younger white man, about 30 years old. This one seemed to be stretching and preening.

Mac told Johnny about four kinds of boats employed by the local salmon fishing fleet: purse seines, gill-net boats, trawlers and tenders. The latter tended reef-net boats. Aside from fishing boats, there were many pleasure yachts at Squalicum Harbor, including about 200 live-aboard yachtsmen.

Mac pointed out the *Rainbow Ferry*, capable of holding two or three cars or one semi-trailer truck. The *Rainbow Ferry* served such destinations as Blakely Island, which had a small airport but no service from the Washington State Ferry system. Mac, Dirk and Johnny also passed the *Western Gulf*, an oil-spill skimmer.

From the marina they could see a cement plant on the bluff overlooking the bay. Mac said houses near the cement plant used to be a uniform white from cement dust. The three men also could see the Bacon House on the bluff. Architect Henry Bacon, who designed the Lincoln Memorial in Washington, D.C., also designed the Bacon House in Bellingham for his cousin George.

Also visible was an elegant, brick Victorian city hall, built in 1893 in what is now downtown Bellingham. This building had become the Whatcom Museum of History and Art.

Now the three men entered the private docks where Dirk's father kept an old cabin cruiser, christened *The Masquerader*.

Johnny was particularly interested in an antique motor vessel. Although its design bore elegant lines, it appeared to be a small military ship. It had a very small mast, which Dirk figured was primarily a stabilizer. The only name on the boat was on the stern, and Dirk had to stand at the end of the dock and lean over the water in order to read the name.

"Don't fall in," Mac warned.

"I think it's name is *Sans Souci*," Dirk reported.

A nearby boater was washing his yacht, and Dirk asked him whether he knew anything about the *Sans Souci*.

"The name is French for 'without a care.' I don't know who owns it," the boater said. "I've never seen anyone onboard. I found an article on

Wikipedia about a boat that very much resembles this one, called the *USS Sans Souci II*. It was built in Seattle as a civilian yacht but was requisitioned to serve in the Puget Sound as a Navy patrol boat and a destroyer tender during World War I."

"I'll bet there is a lot of history behind this collection of yachts at the marina here," Dirk remarked. "It's like a museum. You couldn't say that about your average parking lot full of cars."

"Yeah. Boats usually last longer than cars," the other man agreed.

Mac and Dirk carried Johnny and his wheelchair, separately, aboard *The Masquerader*, where Dirk offered Mac a beer from his father's refrigerator in the galley. He was not sure whether Johnny should drink alcohol, although the guy certainly was of legal age. Without giving it a whole lot of thought, he handed a beer to Johnny, too.

Dirk and Mac talked while Johnny sipped his beer, gradually becoming more sociable. Johnny complained that the company from which his mother had bought their van had not shown them everything they needed to know in order to operate the van.

Shortly after they acquired the van, Johnny and his mother had driven out to Blaine to see a friend. They had left the side door of the van open, with the ramp out, for about three hours while they visited the friend. When John and his mother were ready to leave, the battery of the van was dead. Leaving the door open and the ramp out had drained the battery's power. Fortunately the friend owned a battery charger.

The alcohol relaxed Johnny to the point that he felt comfortable discussing the injury that changed his life. He volunteered the information that when he had been a freshman he had walked into a room at his fraternity just as a drunken young woman was swinging a golf club in the room. Johnny turned away from the swing but the club hit Johnny in the small of his back.

Mac reacted to this revelation by placing his hand to his forehead. His chin fell and his shoulders slumped. Later he explained to Dirk that Johnny's account of his injury had shocked Mac so much that he was in pain.

"You have too much empathy," Dirk suggested.

"I don't think I have too much empathy," Mac responded. "We are in trouble if we lose our empathy, in my opinion."

"I should have said you have a lot of empathy, not too much," Dirk said.

But it was Johnny, not Mac, who was in trouble at the moment aboard *The Masquerader*. Johnny suddenly was unconscious and was having difficulty breathing.

"Something's wrong with Johnny!" Mac shouted.

They tried to talk to Johnny but he was unresponsive. His skin was cold and sweaty. Johnny started to vomit, and Mac held a salad bowl from the galley under Johnny's face. Dirk decided to call for paramedics. Before the medics arrived, Johnny regained consciousness but was very groggy. Dirk asked him if he knew where he was.

"Bellingham," he replied.

"Where in Bellingham?" Mac asked.

"Dirk's boat," Johnny said.

Dirk tried to persuade Johnny to lie down, but he did not seem interested in lying down, and Mac said they should leave Johnny where he was. Mac went out to the street to meet the firefighters when they arrived.

Three firemen took Johnny's pulse and found it to be much lower than normal. Dirk and Mac explained that the three of them had gone for a long walk, and Johnny had consumed half a beer. The firemen could not believe that Johnny drank only half a beer, but Dirk and Mac insisted that was all he had. The firemen thought Johnny should go to the hospital.

"Or I could go home and rest," Johnny said.

"That would not be a good idea," one of the firemen insisted.

The firemen persuaded Johnny to lie down on the deck, on his side, so that blood could circulate to his brain more easily. Then paramedics arrived. They hoisted Johnny onto a gurney and took him to the big ambulance truck on the street. A tall, handsome man wandered over, and Mac recognized him as an orthopedic surgeon who had treated Mac. He kept a yacht at the marina.

After Mac and Dirk described Johnny's symptoms to the orthopedic surgeon, he said: "Well, I guess there's no need for an orthopedic surgeon here."

The surgeon left as the ambulance drove away. Dirk watched the ambulance for a few seconds, and then watched the orthopedic surgeon. As the surgeon returned to the docks, he waved at a man standing on the deck of an old sailboat. The man waved back. Dirk thought the man looked familiar, but he could not remember how he knew the man.

Mac called Johnny's mother and promised her that Mac and Dirk would follow Johnny to the hospital. She could not go to the hospital because Mac and Dirk had her van, and she seemed confident that they could handle the situation. When they arrived at St. Joseph Hospital they joined the teeming masses in the waiting room. A large woman in a motorized wheelchair, who frequently grimaced in pain, was parked at the front desk with a retinue of relatives.

Soon a clerk at the desk directed Dirk and Mac into the treatment area, through doors that said "do not enter." She must have released the lock remotely. They found some paramedics but these paramedics did not know anything about Johnny; they were not the paramedics who had transported Johnny. Dirk and Mac found Johnny way in the back. He looked fine. He was hooked to an I.V., receiving his second bag of liquids.

A patient in the next bed was snoring loudly, and signals were beeping behind the curtain.

The signals sounded ominous to Dirk, but no medical staff responded. Dirk and Mac waited about 30 minutes for Johnny to finish the I.V. Then the emergency-room physician, a friendly woman, said Johnny was "good to go." He had become dehydrated during the long, busy afternoon, and the small amount of beer he consumed was too much for him, the doctor explained. Now Johnny was rehydrated.

Dirk and Mac took Johnny home to his mother, who was surprisingly calm about the whole incident. She did not blame anyone for Johnny's dehydration, and seemed pleased that Mac and Dirk had been willing to spend some time with her son. She evidently was much accustomed to her son's medical problems.

Dirk and Mac returned to Yew Rock Mobile Home Park. Not until he went to bed did Dirk remember who was the man he had seen waving at the orthopedic surgeon. It was the caretaker at Bay Horizon Park, where Steve Ostrander had been found. The caretaker apparently had a sailboat that was docked in Bellingham. Somehow this seemed significant, but Dirk was slow to understand why.

Chapter 13

When he awakened in the morning, it dawned on him that the Bay Horizon Park caretaker could have whacked Ostrander on the head at the marina, pulled him out of the water and taken him to Bay Horizon Park. Dirk did not even wait to eat breakfast before he called Lt. Davis.

"But what motive would the caretaker have for doing this crime?" Davis pressed.

"He was disappointed that a media circus did not erupt when the body turned up," Dirk offered. "He wanted the public to know about Bay Horizon Park. He wanted to bring the park out of obscurity."

"That really is far-fetched," Davis objected.

Dirk presented his theory to Mac when Mac dropped by for coffee.

"It sounds plausible to me," Mac said. "The caretaker could be seriously twisted. But if the cops don't like it, we need to persuade them with some more credible evidence. In my opinion we should get Isaac drunk and send him out on the docks, while we keep an eye on him, and see what happens. Given another opportunity, the caretaker might strike again."

"That would be too dangerous."

"Those docks are going to remain dangerous to any drunk college kid who stumbles out there until someone finds out who killed Steve Ostrander."

"Why don't you go out on the docks?"

"I don't know how to act drunk," Mac declared. "I've never been drunk in my life. Isaac would be a natural."

"I suppose Isaac could pretend to be drunk," Dirk allowed. "Let's talk to him."

Later they broached their idea to Isaac.

"I'll do it but only if I really am drunk," Isaac said. "We have to make it fun."

Dirk made a run to a grocery store for vodka and Kaluha, because Isaac's favorite drink was the black Russian. He also stopped at a marijuana store — legal in Washington State since 2014. After showing his driver's license to an employee at the door, and again to the cashier, he bought a small package of pre-rolled cigarettes. No one had asked for his I.D. when he bought alcohol.

Isaac began drinking at 9 p.m. at Dirk's place. Mac and Dirk remained completely sober in case they had to rescue Isaac. They sat in the breakfast nook, fine-tuning their plans for the evening as Isaac finished his first drink.

As he began his second drink, Isaac wanted to hear some stories from Dirk and Mac about their youthful misadventures with alcohol and/or testosterone flooding their blood vessels.

"One of the most stupid things I did was with a friend in California when I was visiting there," Dirk said. "His parents lived on a small island in Newport Harbor, south of Los Angeles. My friend and I took his parent's yacht into the ocean one night. The ocean down there is a lot different than here in Bellingham. We have so many islands outside Bellingham Bay. But down there, it's open sea as soon as you leave Newport Harbor.

"After we cleared the jetties of the harbor, my friend turned on the automatic pilot. We went below to have some beer and smoke some pot. After a while, we went upstairs to the deck to check on things. The boat had turned itself around and was heading back toward the harbor. We were only a few hundred yards from crashing into the rock jetty. My friend took manual control of the boat, and steered it away from the rocks.

"It was foolhardy enough that we had set the auto pilot and then gone below deck, because we were still near the harbor and there could have been other boats in the area. Probably other skippers would have seen us and avoided us, but you never know. But for the auto pilot to reverse course like that was really dangerous. We probably would have survived a crash into the rock jetty, but we would have destroyed the yacht. His parents would have been furious."

"That's a good story," Isaac remarked. "It's your turn, Mac."

"I never got stinking drunk but I did some stupid things," Mac conceded. "When I was 15 years old my friends and I would steal our parents' cars at night. We would take the keys and push the car away from the house so the parents would not hear the engine start. Then we would drive all over the place, even though we barely knew how to drive. We would drive on the wrong side of the road. We would drive with our headlights turned off. We would speed. Sometimes we took off our clothes and drove naked. We never got caught. Luckily we never hurt anyone.

"It's a wonder that anyone survives adolescence," Mac added.

Isaac poured himself a third drink.

"When I was 20, I went flying in a small plane with a friend my age who just got his solo pilot's license," Isaac recalled. "I took a joint with me and smoked part of it while we flew over the San Juan Islands. We flew low over the water and high over Mount Constitution. I loved it. My friend did not smoke the joint but who knows how much he was affected by second-hand inhalation. When we returned to the airport, he came in too low. He had to pull up or the wheels would have hit the grass instead of the pavement. He revved the engine and we started to climb. At that point, he should have gone around for another landing attempt. But he lowered the rpm and put the plane down. I thought we would crash. We were going too fast when we touched down. We raced past the first turn-off. We sped past another turn-off. My friend finally brought the plane to a stop at the very end of the runway. I was scared but I just laughed it off."

"On a lighter note," Dirk began another story, "I was out in Bellingham Bay once in a small speedboat. There was a full moon. We had some beer and pot with us and we were having a grand time. There were two couples on board. My friend's hat blew into the water. We had been following a path of moonlight reflecting off the water, so I turned the boat around and followed the path back to where we had been. We found the hat! My friend was from Iowa, and he thought it was amazing that we could find his hat in the huge Pacific Ocean, as he called it, although we were only in Bellingham Bay."

By midnight, Isaac was hammered. Dirk drove to the marina, with Mac in the front passenger seat and Isaac in the backseat. They let Isaac out at the docks. Isaac wandered amid the yachts in a disoriented zigzag manner. Dirk and Mac followed at a discreet distance. Dirk began to worry that this was another stupid shenanigan from his careless adolescence. The docks were not well lit and there was no moon. What if Isaac fell into the water? What if someone pushed him? What if someone hit Isaac in the head before Dirk and Mac had a chance to intervene? What were they doing out on the deserted docks at midnight on a moonless night?

After about 30 minutes on the docks, a shadowy figure approached Isaac. Dirk's heart began to beat fast. He and Mac moved quickly to close the gap between Isaac and them. The shadowy figure grasped Isaac. Adrenalin surged through Dirk and he outpaced Mac as they ran.

"Stop!" he shouted.

"You stop," the shadowy figure responded, while shining a flashlight into Dirk's eyes. "Just hold it right there."

"What are you doing?" Dirk demanded.

"I'm arresting a drunken kid," the other man answered, "for his own good."

"You're a cop?" Dirk asked.

"Oh, great, the cops are here," Mac groaned. "What a mess."

"Do you know this kid?" asked the uniformed Bellingham cop.

"Yes, he's our friend. My dad has a boat here and my friend had a little too much to drink, and we thought he should walk it off. But we were watching him so he'd be safe."

"We got a call from a boater about a drunk stumbling around on the docks," the officer noted. "We've had some dangerous incidents with drunken college kids out here."

"If you will allow us, we will take care of Isaac," Dirk said. "There's been no harm done."

"I'd say there's been harm to some of his brain cells. Have you been drinking, too?"

"No."

"What about you?" the officer asked Mac, while pointing his flashlight at Mac.

"No, sir. I don't drink alcohol."

"Well, neither of you smell of alcohol, but why is your friend so drunk?"

"He broke up with his girlfriend," Dirk ad-libbed. "He wanted to get hammered and we wanted to keep an eye on him, so we brought him here to my dad's boat. We will be sure to get him home safely."

"Alright, do that. Do it straight away."

The officer checked their identification, wrote down their names and escorted the three miscreants to Dirk's car, and Dirk drove back to Yew Rock Mobile Home Park. Mac and Dirk put Isaac to bed in the guestroom of Dirk's home.

Richard Howland

Chapter 14

I saac was still asleep when Lt. Davis called.

"I have a report on my desk that says you and two other clowns were out on the docks last night," Davis growled to Dirk. "I don't have to think too hard to know what you were doing. You were trying to flush out a killer. That was dumb."

"Well, yeah, it was kind of dumb," Dirk said. "We sometimes get a little too enthusiastic about helping our law enforcement pals."

"You shouldn't hang out with that nutcase Mac Martino," Davis scolded. "He's a bad influence on you. And this young guy, Isaac Casey: He shouldn't be hanging out with you. And he definitely shouldn't be hanging out with Abigail Baker."

"Why not? What do you know about her?"

"I'm investigating a suspicious death," Davis reminded Dirk. "And she's a person of interest."

"Abigail is a suspect?"

"Just tell your pal Isaac to stay away from her. She might be dangerous. She has a history of stalking her ex-boyfriends. And how did Isaac get involved with her? I have no doubt that you put him up to it."

At that, Davis hung up.

A few minutes later, Mac showed up for coffee.

"Davis wants us to quit playing detective," Dirk told Mac.

Dirk repeated the main points of his conversation with Lt. Davis.

Mac responded, "You have to ask yourself: Why did Davis tell you that Abigail might be a suspect? Wouldn't he keep that to himself ordinarily? In my opinion, he wanted to plant a seed in your mind. He wants Isaac to tease out some useful information from Abigail. But Davis can't tell you that directly. You're a civilian and Isaac is a civilian. It might be a little dangerous. So Davis doesn't say anything directly. He just plants the seed of an idea in your head. That's my opinion."

Isaac stumbled out of bed as Mac was presenting his theory. Isaac heard only the last part.

"What might be a little dangerous?" he asked. "What seed is Davis planting? Let me have some coffee. I'm really hung over."

Dirk poured a cup of coffee and filled a pitcher with water. He set the pitcher beside the coffee.

"You need to hydrate yourself," he told Isaac. "Don't listen to Mac. He just wants to get you into more trouble than you were in last night."

"I don't remember getting into any trouble. It was fun talking to you guys about all the screw-ups in your past."

"Last night was another screw-up," Dirk commented.

"Why don't you take it easy for a few days," Mac said to Isaac. "Then you can invite Abigail to lunch aboard *The Masquerader*. Tell her you want her to meet Dirk and me because we are good friends. We will steer the conversation to her obsession with Steve Ostrander, and see how she reacts. Lt. Davis thinks she was stalking him and might have killed him. If she couldn't have him, no one was going to have him. In my opinion she could have hit him on the head or pushed him into the water. Then she dragged him to her car and drove him to that park — in my opinion."

"She is a little off kilter," Isaac said. "Maybe she did it."

Richard Howland

Chapter 15

Their plan went well at first. Isaac and Abigail showed up aboard *The Masquerader* at the appointed time. Dirk prepared salmon with an herb paste, made of green onions, dried dill, olive oil and salt. He oiled a rack and placed the salmon on the rack in a tray holding water. While his guests sipped wine, he baked the salmon for 25 minutes. He also stir-fried some zucchini and mushrooms.

Mac waited until they were done eating before he started talking about Steve Ostrander.

"Isaac tells me you knew the boy," Mac said.

Abigail spoke easily of Ostrander until Mac confronted her more directly.

"I've heard from other people, not Isaac, mind you, that you were obsessed with Steve," he declared.

"Why would anyone say that?" Abigail replied.

"In my opinion, maybe you were stalking him."

"I followed him a few times for his own good, to look after him."

"You followed him from Ellensburg to Bellingham for his own good?"

Dirk and Isaac, tongue-tied, looked on apprehensively as Abigail grew visibly angry.

"This is none of your business," she said sternly.

"It's my business if you hurt my friend Isaac," Mac insisted. "Maybe you killed Steve in a jealous rage and you might do the same thing to Isaac."

Dirk nearly had found his voice and was going to intervene. He thought he ought to say something like: "Now, Mac, Abigail is a guest aboard *The Masquerader* and we don't grill our guests."

But before Dirk could speak, Abigail grabbed a filet knife from the galley and brandished it.

"Shut up, old man," she shouted.

Mac pulled out a handgun, which served to shut up Abigail.

Dirk finally found his voice.

"You brought a gun? I do not want guns aboard this boat," Dirk blurted.

"It's a good thing I brought my gun. She has a knife!"

"I didn't even know you owned a gun!"

"You always say I'm a hoarder. I have everything I could ever need, you always say. And right now I need a gun."

"Is it loaded?"

"Of course it's loaded!"

Abigail bolted out of the cabin, and Dirk called the police. A patrol car must have been nearby because it responded quickly enough to arrive at the entrance to the gangways just as Abigail got there. She retreated onto the docks and headed to the old sailboat where Dirk once had seen the caretaker of Bay Horizon Park. She climbed aboard the sailboat and entered the cabin.

Mac stayed aboard *The Masquerader*, keeping himself and his gun out of view.

Soon the docks were crowded with cops, and Lt. Davis arrived. Dirk explained what had happened aboard *The Masquerader*, and he pointed out the sailboat where he had last seen Abigail. Dirk told Davis that he had seen the park caretaker on this boat earlier. Davis shouted at Abigail, ordering her to come out.

Abigail did exit the cabin, but she remained on the sailboat, holding the knife.

"I did not kill Steven. This old man did it," Abigail announced, gesturing toward the cabin. "He's inside that cabin."

"She's lying," said Paul Cronn, caretaker of Bay Horizon Park, as he emerged from the cabin. "She killed the kid and she paid me to get rid of the body."

"How do you two know each other?" Davis demanded.

"I just happened to be on the docks when she knocked the kid into the water," Cronn declared. "I saw it happen. Then she saw me watching, and she offered me $5,000 to pull the guy out of the water and take him somewhere out of town."

"Why did you dump his body at Bay Horizon Park?" Davis asked.

"I know my way around that park," Cronn explained. "Most people don't go out there, and no one was likely to see me."

Abigail brandished the knife and moved closer to Cronn. A K-9 sergeant released his dog, and the dog bounded aboard the sailboat, grasping Abigail's wrist and forcing her to drop the knife. Officers swarmed aboard the boat and handcuffed both suspects.

"You had better hope that your pal has a permit for that gun," Davis said to Dirk. "He's as crazy as Abigail. Your friend Isaac is crazy, too. All three of you are crazy."

"We're good citizens is all," Dirk said.

Interview with the author

What inspired you to write *The Disconcerting Concert*?

I attended a concert where my mind drifted away from the music and I started to wonder about where page turners come from and who they are.

How did you select a title?

While I was writing it, I was going to call it *The Page Turner*, but I checked online and I found there already was a book by that title, written by David Leavitt and published in 1998, about an affair between a young page turner and his older pianist idol. So I tried to come up with another title. I like to have fun with alliteration and puns, so I played around with the word "concert" for a while, and I came up with *A Disconcerting Concert*. I looked up that and all I found was a chapter called "The Disconcerting Concert Party" in *Propeller Island*, a Jules Verne science-fiction novel about a string quartet on a huge ship, published in 1905.

Did you know what the ending would be when you started to write?

No. I created a group of suspects, each of whom

could have done the crime, but I did not decide who the killer was until I was nearly finished with writing the novel.

How did you get into writing?

Initially and essentially I was and am an avid reader. Reading introduces you to a wider world, and authors become your mentors and idols. I think it is a natural progression for a reader to aspire to be a writer. But I don't really like that term, "writer." It sounds pretentious. After all, most of us read and write. I prefer a more specific term, such as "author" or "novelist." You could substitute "biographer" or "historian" or "newspaperman" or "freelance journalist." I became a newspaperman after college when I got a job as a copyboy at a daily paper. A copyboy basically is a go-fer or errand boy. I went all over the five-story building where I worked, learning how a newspaper was put together. We put out five editions each day, and I went downstairs to the presses to pick up each edition that came out during my shift. I ferried photographs from the library to the newsroom. I went upstairs to the composing room on various missions. I hunted down reporters in the cafeteria when a source or a wife was trying to reach them. I went looking for copy editors in the tavern across the street when their bosses wondered where they had gone. The city editors eventually offered me a summer internship as a reporter, and eventually they hired me as a reporter. I liked the weekly paycheck so I stayed with it for three decades. I did not write books until I retired. The life of a freelance journalist or novelist, without a steady paycheck, was too scary for me.

How do you get your work into print?

I took a two-night course at Whatcom Community College about self-publishing. The instructor referred class members to Applied Digital Imaging, a print shop in Bellingham. I went there and they referred me to a local book designer, Kate Weisel, who put my first book together and has continued to do so for my second and third books. It does not cost a lot. Self-publishing also is available online. The Internet has devalued the work of songwriters and journalists, to the point where most people expect music and news to be free. So it is harder to earn a living as a musician or author. But the Internet has made it easier for people to express themselves if they do not expect much monetary compensation.

Do you have a writing routine?

No. I write whenever I feel like it, wherever it's convenient. I take notes (by hand) wherever I go. Usually I write on a laptop in the kitchen whenever I have some time available. I spend more time writing my journal than working on my books, but a lot of material from my journal gets into my novels. I make an entry in my journal only when something interesting happens, not every day.

How is writing a novel different from writing for a newspaper?

Newspaper articles are much shorter and usually appear in print a day or two after you start writing. There is instant gratification in that you do not have to wait months or years to see your work in print. But you do not have much opportunity to rewrite. Writing for a daily newspaper is a much more social experience than writing a novel. I worked in a crowded, noisy newsroom with fellow reporters all around me, making phone calls and chatting with one another. On other floors there were printers, pressmen, ad salesmen, customer-service representatives and others, who wandered into the newsroom from time to time for meetings or just to socialize. I often worked with any one of about 10 staff photographers on a story assignment, or sometimes with a freelance photographer. On big stories, two, three or more reporters might work together.

Which living writers inspire you?

Ann Patchett is one of my heroes. Not only do I thoroughly enjoy her novels, but I respect her so much for investing in a bricks-and-mortar bookstore. She is the co-owner of Parnassus Books in Nashville. What a great gift that is to readers, writers and publishers. She is actively trying to reverse the decline in recent years of the book business. And I love Richard Russo's work. I've never read anything by Anne Tyler or Elizabeth George that I did not enjoy. John Irving and Howard Norman are two more favorites.

Which genres do you enjoy the most? And the least?

I read mysteries, thrillers, biographies, history and "great literature." I enjoy just about everything other than poetry. When poets decided they did not need to rhyme, poetry lost its point, for me anyway. As a newspaperman, I was trained to make my prose crystal clear to the reader. Poets are too obscure for my tastes.

The novels I've written fall, I believe, into a genre that has been called the "polite country house mystery." My stories do not take place entirely in the countryside, but they are mostly polite and are set in a small city. I'm not into extreme brutal violence. I hate stories about serial killers because I cannot identify with serial killers. I can identify with someone who kills once in a rage or for spectacular personal gain, and perhaps kills again in order to escape being caught. But to kill for the sheer pleasure of killing? Such killers exist but I don't want anything to do with them.

Which authors or books do you consider to be overrated? Have you left books unfinished?

I never finished *To the Lighthouse*, by Virginia Woolf. I just was not motivated enough to slog through it. I also failed to get further than 50 pages into *Gravity's Rainbow*, by Thomas Pynchon.

There was just too much descriptive detail. I knew every tree on the block and every crack in the sidewalk, but I did not know who the main character was, the geographic locale or the time period, and I had no idea what the story was about. I prefer a compelling narrative rather than copious description. I was forced to read James Joyce while in high school, and I probably was not mature enough to appreciate him, but he turned me off so thoroughly at a young age that I have avoided most books about Ireland ever since. I tried to read Charles Bukowski because so many people think he was so cool, but his writing is so dreary and depressing. I couldn't take it. Life is short. If I am not enjoying a book or learning a lot, I feel no compulsion to finish it.

Are the characters in your novels based on real people?

In some respects my characters are composites of people I know. I might take a personality characteristic from one friend or relative and add to it a characteristic from another friend or relative, combining the characteristics in one fictional character. But I put my characters into imagined situations that none of my friends or relatives have encountered precisely. My characters are in part inspired by people I know, but no one I know appears in my fiction exactly as who they are in real life.

Are you working on a new book?

I think my next novel will be about a murder in a public garden. The inspiration comes from a walk in a garden in Seattle with friends. We walked through a spooky, thickly forested section of the garden. This section originally had been a tree farm for a gardening company. The owner of the company gradually developed a show garden around the tree farm. One friend said I could set my next murder mystery in the garden. Another friend suggested a title for the mystery. As we left the old tree farm, I found an empty cigarette pack with Chinese characters printed on it. This cigarette pack could be a clue to the murder, I told my friends.

After our walk, we found a nearby restaurant for lunch. One friend mentioned that her husband's sister barely could walk at a graduation ceremony, and I asked whether that was why this friend, who lived in California, was in Seattle: To attend a graduation?

"I'm here to say goodbye," my friend said bluntly.

She explained that her oncologist had done a brain scan and had told my friend that she had only about three months to live. As her appointment with the oncologist had ended, the doctor and the nurse had hugged my friend, which was the first time they had done that.

When she went to her pharmacist after the doctor's appointment, the pharmacist handed her a plastic bag full of drugs. My friend thought there had been a mistake, and she tried to give back the bag. The pharmacist called it a "comfort bag." It contained morphine and other powerful drugs for various symptoms, including nausea.

After we returned to the garden so my friend and her husband could get their rental car, my friend said she wanted to pray. We huddled and she thanked God for giving her good friends. She thanked me for having more confidence in her than she had in herself when she was a newsroom clerk and I sent her to cover a truck that fell from an elevated freeway and crashed into a house in California early one morning — an incident that resulted in her only Page 1 byline. She thanked God for giving me new friends in Bellingham. She asked God to look after me.

She was praying for me, at a time when I would have thought I should have been praying for her. We hugged, and she and her husband drove away.

I want to dedicate my next book to her.

About the Author

Richard S. Howland worked for a daily newspaper in California for 31 years as a reporter, editor and book reviewer. He now lives in Bellingham, Washington. His first published novels were ***The Samaritan Trap*** and ***Yew Rock***.